COLD-HEARTED CORPSE

A Booker Falls Mystery

KENN GRIMES

*For my good friend,
Carole Chirgwin
Hope you enjoy this Northern
Michigan mystery!
Kenn Grimes*

This book is fiction. All characters, events, and organizations portrayed in this novel are the product of the author's imagination or are used fictitiously. Any resemblance to actual persons—living or dead—is entirely coincidental.

Copyright © 2021 by Kenn Grimes

All rights reserved. No parts of this book may be reproduced or transmitted in any form or by any means, electronic or mechanical, including photocopying, recording or by any information storage and retrieval system, without written permission from the author, except for the inclusion of brief quotations in a review.

For information, email Cozy Cat Press at:
cozycatpress@gmail.com
or visit our website at:
www.cozycatpress.com

ISBN: 978-1-952579-30-1

Printed in the United States of America

10 9 8 7 6 5 4 3 2 1

DEDICATION

For my granddaughters,
Hope Elizabeth (Grimes) Hutchison
and
Alayna Marie Lofgren
both of whom, like Myrtle,
are strong, independent, women who
have made their own way in life
and
of whom I am exceedingly proud.

ACKNOWLEDGEMENTS

When I send my manuscript out to my pre-publication readers, I always wonder how they could possibly find anything to tell me that would improve what I consider a perfect novel. Somehow, they never fail to reveal the fallacy of my thinking and show no reticence in making spot-on suggestions and pointing out my myriad errors. So, my warmest thanks go out to Linda Miller, Nancy Gall-Clayton, and my wife, Judy, and special thanks to my editor, Madge Walls, as well as my publisher, Patricia Rockwell, owner of Cozy Cat Press.

CHAPTER ONE

Myrtle studied the image of the woman in the white dress staring back at her from the cheval mirror. Was this the same woman who had arrived in Booker Falls nearly three years ago? A few pounds heavier, due to the more than adequate—not to mention, scrumptious—meals Mrs. Darling provided at the boarding house where Myrtle lived.

"We'll put some meat on dose bones while you're here," her landlady had told her that first day.

And, notwithstanding the dress she now had on—definitely not her normal, everyday wear—Myrtle's sense of clothing style had improved considerably, thanks to the efforts of both her best friend and housemate, Daisy O'Hearn, and Isabell Dougherty, the proprietor of Première Qualité Women's Wear.

She'd not completely forsaken the cap and green-and-black plaid trousers she'd worn when she first came to town, attire which gave her the appearance of a newsboy sorely in need of a haircut; but her wardrobe had expanded significantly in a more fashionable way beyond that.

Three years. It felt like she'd been a part of the community much longer than that.

She still remembered her first day.

It was almost a disaster.

She had driven thirteen hundred miles in fifteen days, a journey that took her from New Orleans to Michigan's Keweenaw Peninsula, where she was to begin her new job as assistant librarian at Adelaide College.

Motoring into town in her twelve-year-old maroon Model N Ford, she was surprised at how tall a number of the buildings were, some as many as four stories. She'd been told Michigan's Upper Peninsula was at the top of the world and that the Keweenaw Peninsula was ever farther north than that. She expected to find the populace living in tents or lean-tos or, at best, ramshackle homes, with wild animals——maybe even wolves——roaming the streets.

But this had been a real town, with wood and brick buildings and a macadam street, a relief from the dusty roads she'd been traveling.

And there were no wild animals—only ordinary people going about their business, strolling up and down the wooden sidewalks, entering and leaving the various businesses. Good Lord—there was even a bookstore!

She had driven by J. P. Finnegan's Fancy Groceries and Fresh Meats, L. L. Reynolds' Funeral Parlor, the Salle de Spectacle Theater, the Booker Falls Bank & Trust, and Miss Madeline's Eatery where she slowed down to make sure she'd read the sign correctly on the adjacent building: The Polar Bear Ice Cream Parlor!

Further down the street, she'd driven past Booker Falls' two churches: St. James Lutheran Church on the right and a much larger, finer, church on the left——St. Barbara Catholic Church.

But it was the two-story, double-bay fire station that almost did her in.

So intent was she on studying its imposing tower, that she hadn't noticed the horse and carriage coming around the corner until the voice of its driver rang out.

"Whoa! Whoa, Jessie!"

She had nearly run over the county constable, Henri de la Cruz.

An unpleasant exchange of words followed but, despite that ill-fated beginning, the two eventually became not only good friends but romantically involved. She had even helped him solve five murders, including a triple homicide—not that he necessarily welcomed her assistance.

Henri wasn't her only suitor.

Before she even made her way through town, she had encountered George Salmon, the town mayor. The following day George stopped by the boarding house to ask her to the ice cream social at the Lutheran church. Myrtle had declined then but, over time, as with Henri, she had grown fond of George and accepted other invitations.

This past Valentine's Day both men had made known their intentions by asking for her hand in marriage.

Three years ago when she first arrived in Booker Falls, marriage was the farthest thing from her mind.

Now, here it was: her wedding day.

*****

St. Barbara Catholic Church served the spiritual needs of scores of miners who called Booker Falls home, along with the rest of the Catholic population in the area.

At a cost of fifty thousand dollars, the building, constructed of Jacobsville sandstone mined from a nearby town of the same name and completed in 1892, was older than most of the other churches in the area. The steeple, which held a huge bell, soared seventy-five feet into the sky, towering over every other building in town.

Inside, a curved cathedral ceiling rose forty feet above the main floor. A fifteen-foot-long crucifix hung suspended from it above the altar. Statues of Joseph and Mary occupied a niche on one side of the circular chancel while one of St. Barbara, the patron saint of miners, graced the opposite side. The pulpit, elevated eight feet, allowed the priest to keep a watchful eye on any congregant who might doze off during the sermon.

At the rear of the sanctuary, the balcony held a choir loft and a four-hundred-pipe organ with ten ranks.

On most Saturday mornings the church was empty, quiet, and dark as a tomb. Other than the sanctuary lamp, the only light was that which made its way through the stained glass windows, casting a multi-colored display across the maple pews. Father Fabian would be in the rectory next door, writing his sermon for the following day.

Not this Saturday morning.

Not only were the lights all on, but lit candles also adorned with flowers graced the end of each pew. More flowers—roses, tulips, hydrangeas, peonies, buttercups—covered the chancel area.

Mrs. Carlisle, head of the altar guild, was busy arranging the communion ware while ushers at the rear of the sanctuary directed arriving guests to one side of the aisle or the other.

Father Fabian *was* in the rectory, patiently waiting for the appointed time of the ceremony he was about to officiate. Normally, he put his vestments on in the sacristy but today he had graciously offered the room to Myrtle as a dressing room.

*****

"You almost ready?"

Myrtle turned and saw Daisy standing in the doorway.

"I've changed my mind," said Myrtle.

"Like he——like heck you have," said Daisy, remembering

she was in a church.

Myrtle smiled. "Just kidding. Don't worry—I'm going through with it."

"Willingly, I hope. I still can't believe you're getting married before me."

"Do you have to wait until Eddie retires before you can get married?"

"He's the fire chief, so he has to live at the station. I'm not living at any fire station until he steps down next year—June first."

"And you're getting married on the second?"

Daisy laughed. "No reason to wait around. I just can't get over your dress."

Initially, Myrtle had planned to wear a simple white dress for the ceremony; but when Isabell showed her a picture of the dress in *Vogue* magazine, she was hooked.

Floor-length and fashioned in silk organza over silk georgette, the dress was form-fitting to the knees with a slightly flared hem, a deep V-neck, and draped flutter sleeves. White opera-length, kidskin gloves lined in silk covered Myrtle's arms to just above her elbows.

A dazzling tiara and crystal chandelier earrings completed the ensemble.

"I'm sure yours will be just as beautiful," said Myrtle.

Daisy nodded. "I hope so. But I sure won't look as good in it. Kid, you're gonna knock 'em dead."

She turned and headed for the door. "See you out there."

*****

As the first strains of Mendelssohn's Wedding March filled the church, the ushers opened the rear double doors.

Myrtle stood, as transfixed now as she had been earlier looking at herself in the mirror.

She watched the guests slowly rise to their feet and turn to face her.

Waiting inside, at the end of the aisle down which she was about to walk, was the wedding party: Mrs. Darling, Daisy, Henri, and Pierre—her housemates at the boarding house; George Salmon, the town's mayor, Eddie O'Halloran, the town's fire chief and Daisy's fiancé; Jake McIntyre, the county prosecutor; Paige Turner, owner of the local bookstore; and Lydia Plummer, who had taken Myrtle's place as assistant librarian when Myrtle was promoted after the death of her boss—the most recent murder in which she'd been involved.

Myrtle felt every eye focused on her.

And they may have been.

But the question on the minds of every guest was: who was the handsome stranger by her side?

CHAPTER TWO

FIVE MONTHS EARLIER

Myrtle inhaled deeply, then let her breath out and watched it float off into the frigid air, hang suspended for a few seconds, and vanish.

She jammed her gloved hands deeper into the pockets of her skunk-skin coat; it was perfect for today's weather with the temperature straining to hit double digits. Three feet of snow covered the ground. Myrtle had purchased the coat a few years back when she and Daisy took a road trip to Red Jacket.

Daisy thought she was crazy for buying a coat made from the skins of such loathsome creatures.

"It's going to stink to high heaven," she'd said.

But it didn't. It was warm and everybody commented on it—usually favorably.

Today, with the snow coming down, it showed more white than usual.

Myrtle's head was covered by a full fur Russian hat. Even

though she wore earmuffs underneath it, her ears still felt a bit tingly.

She stared at the grave marker in front of her, the one she and Mrs. Darling had picked out from the Sears and Roebuck catalog. Constructed of White Acme Rutland Italian Marble, it stood two feet high. Today, snow covered the bottom portion so that all that was visible was the name at the top: ADOLPH PFROMMER. But Myrtle knew what was engraved on the rest of the stone: 1840-1921 and the inscription chosen by Mrs. Darling which read: A GOOD FRIEND. REST IN PEACE.

A marker so nice was only possible because Mr. Pfrommer had, unknowingly, paid for it himself. He had bequeathed his valuable collection of antique watches to Myrtle, who sold them to Mr. Abramovitz, owner of the local pawn shop. She used the funds to pay for the old man's funeral and this headstone.

A hundred thoughts swirled through her head, not the least of which was: why was she standing here in freezing weather paying her respects to the man who tried to murder her?

"Cold, ain't it?"

Myrtle turned to look at Mrs. Darling, who stood next to her, bundled up in a rabbit fur coat, a chook pulled down over her head, a heavy scarf wrapped around her neck.

Ah, yes—this was why she was here. Her landlady had wanted Myrtle to accompany her to the township cemetery to place a single flower on Mr. Pfrommer's grave. Of course, the temperature being what it was, the flower would probably freeze before the two of them ever left the grounds.

Myrtle had taken the day off from her job as head librarian at the Adelaide College Library and she and Mrs. Darling had set out early in the morning. It took them over an hour and a half of slogging through deep snow to get to the cemetery from the boarding house. Myrtle suspected it would take her and her seventy-year-old companion considerably longer to return.

She was grateful they were wearing snowshoes.

"He wasn't really a bad man, you know," said Mrs. Darling.

Myrtle nodded; she only half-agreed with her landlady's judgment.

Mr. Pfrommer had been a resident at Mrs. Darling's Boarding House when Myrtle arrived in 1919 and had been there far longer than the other two boarders, Henri and Daisy. In his late seventies, he was quiet and withdrawn, though he and Myrtle developed a friendship, taking occasional walks accompanied by Myrtle's dog, Penrod.

Mr. Pfrommer had always been particular that meals be served on time, especially dinner at five o'clock. Following that meal, he would retire to his room, take out his violin, and promptly begin to play for an hour, primarily music by German composers. Afterward, he prepared his nightly libation of absinthe, then sank into his easy chair to read and drink until he fell asleep around nine.

Later he would rise and go to bed.

He'd come to America in 1879 at the age of thirty-nine and had resided for ten years in Quebec before moving to Booker Falls. For the next twenty-three years, he labored as a watchmaker until his employer died and he found himself involuntarily retired.

Soon after arriving in Booker Falls and beginning her job as assistant librarian at the library, Myrtle came across a cache of letters received by a young girl twenty-eight years earlier, shortly before she was murdered. She'd been found strangled to death in the stacks of the library.

Myrtle had turned the letters over to Henri, the county

constable but, inquisitive as she was—the term used by Henri was 'nosy'—had inserted herself into the investigation. Her sleuthing led her to believe the murderer was none other than her housemate, Mr. Pfrommer, and that he was also responsible for another murder back in Quebec.

When Mr. Pfrommer found Myrtle snooping around in his room, he tried to strangle her but was thwarted by George, who had come to the house to see Henri.

Following his trial, Mr. Pfrommer received a life sentence to be served at the prison in Marquette. On Myrtle's first visit there with Mrs. Darling, he had apologized for trying to kill her and for poisoning Penrod in an attempt to scare her off.

Fortunately, Penrod survived.

A year later, Mr. Pfrommer passed away.

Today, January 26, 1922, was the first anniversary of his death.

Myrtle had just looked up to glimpse a bald eagle circling overhead when she felt Mrs. Darling's hand at her elbow.

"You ready to go, dearie? I'm gettin' cold."

"Yes," said Myrtle, "me, too. Let's go."

It was snowing harder now.

CHAPTER THREE

The Annual Chili-Cook-Off had been a Booker Falls institution for almost a quarter-century.

In 1897, followers of the Lutheran faith residing in the town and surrounding areas decided to construct a house of worship. They soon realized that while the manpower to build the church was readily available, the funds necessary to purchase the needed material were lacking. Most of the faithful were miners and loggers, fortunate to bring home enough pay to put food on their tables.

They decided to raise funds by holding a chili cook-off, where people paid to taste and vote on the different entries.

Rules were set. Only wild game could be used; nothing domesticated—no beef, pork, or poultry. The game had to come from Michigan. Eagle meat was forbidden as eagles were sacred to the Indians plus it was America's national bird. Only men could enter the contest—and they had to prepare the chili themselves.

Over the years a handful of entries were disqualified for various reasons, two of which occurred in 1903. The first was Peter Trembley's which included wolverine meat. Peter objected vigorously when told that no wolverines had been sighted in Michigan in forty years.

"Den why's it called da Wolverine State?" asked Peter. "Tell me dat."

No one could answer his question, but the decision still stood.

The other was when Milford Whitman accused Hoppy Pfaulman of stealing his cow and passing it off as elk meat in his chili. The matter was initially resolved when Arès Patja was called in to sample the dish. Arès enjoyed a reputation for being able to identify the species of any prepared meat, be it cooked, broiled, fried, or otherwise.

"Yah, dat's cow for sure," said Arès. "Yah."

The deception was further validated when what remained of the cow was found in Hoppy's barn.

Hoppy spent the next year in jail and missed the Cook-Off.

A new rule was added in 1907. Until then the source of the meat used in the various chilies was not revealed until after the contest was over. But when Ann Marie Worsley and Chuckie Allman died from eating Saul Gorman's offering that turned out to be prepared with owl meat, it was decided that not only must the type of meat be made known ahead of time, but also that the cook who prepared it be required to eat a cup of the concoction before it was made available to others.

If he got sick or died, they wouldn't serve it.

After that, the only problem arose in 1912 when Gaylord Murchinson's skunk chili did not sit well and a half-dozen people got sick.

In the early years, the fee to sample the entries was thirty cents for adults and ten cents for children under twelve. By 1922 it had increased to sixty cents and twenty-five cents for children.

Each person needed to provide his or her own spoon and

container—a bowl or cup or tin can. For the last fifteen years "Grandma" Pierson had sat at the door collecting the money. More than once, when someone appeared without the required funds but who Grandma saw was in need of a good meal, she would wave them on through. If they hadn't thought to bring their own container or spoon, she always had a spare or two in the bag at her feet. All she asked was that they leave them in the kitchen sink when they finished so she could wash them and have them ready for the next person in need.

Originally, the number of cooks was about eight or ten but over time qualifications changed so that by now there were no more than a dozen and a half.

Buckets were placed around the room where the tasters could empty out their containers if they didn't care for the contents. No spitting into the buckets was allowed. Most people carried a second container into which they could expectorate if they needed to.

The aforementioned Milford Whitman, who kept pigs in addition to cows—and indeed was the main provider of pork products to a local eatery known as the Hungry Hog—had a watering tank on the back of his wagon into which he emptied the buckets throughout the day. Afterwards, he transported the slop to his farm and fed it to his livestock.

The winner of the first Cook-Off in 1897 was bobcat chili, prepared by Daniel Ostrander, chief cook at Number Two logging camp located fifteen miles north of Booker Falls. A heated debate followed about whether camp cooks should be allowed to participate, seeing as how they were, technically, professionals. The final verdict was that they should. Since then a number of other camp cooks had submitted their chilies but only one other came in first.

The first four years of the Cook-Off were held in June in the yard behind the church. Then someone reasoned that chili was a delicacy best consumed when it was cold outside. Since the church building had been completed by then, the event was moved inside and to the last Sunday in January, with the whole affair falling under the auspices of the Ladies' Aid Society made up of women from both St. James and St. Barbara's.

The Cook-Off quickly became a popular event, drawing hundreds of people from all over Copper County. In 1911 the newly elected governor, Chase Osborn, and his wife, Lillian, attended, spending the weekend as guests of George Salmon's parents.

Shortly thereafter, the event became a two-day affair, and was scheduled for the last full weekend in January.

While winners in the early years received nothing other than ribbons and accolades, by 1920 the income generated by the Cook-Off had risen to the point where it was decided to award cash prizes to the top three favorites: five dollars for first place, three for second, and one for third.

It was a little after six when George and Myrtle arrived at the church.

Myrtle spotted Daisy at a table with Paige and Saija Albrecht, whose husband, Robert, was the pastor of the congregation.

"I'm going to go see what they've tried so far," said Myrtle.

"Okay. I see Robert. I want to talk with him."

"What all have you tried?" asked Myrtle when she reached the three women.

"I've had squirrel, badger, elk," said Daisy, "and this is— what is this, Saija?"

"Turtle," replied Saija.

"Yeah," said Daisy, "turtle—delicious."

She smacked her lips.

"How about you, Saija?" asked Myrtle.

"Bobcat, elk, and this—turtle, same as Daisy."

"And I've had the same as Saija," said Paige.

"Where's Eddie?" Myrtle asked Daisy. "Is he here?"

"No, somebody had to stay at the fire station and since he's the chief it was him."

"I guess I better get busy if I'm going to catch up with the three of you," said Myrtle.

"Why don't you try the snake?" said Paige. "Let us know what it's like."

Myrtle scrunched up her nose. "Snake? Who would eat snake?"

"Apparently some people," said Daisy. "He's had a big lineup ever since we got here. I'm trying the lynx next."

"Snake," muttered Myrtle, shaking her head and walking off.

In one corner of the room, Joker Mulhearn was dispensing beer from a wooden barrel into Dixie Cups. Everyone knew Joker operated a bar in the back room of Alton Woodruff's barbershop. The beer wasn't free—Joker was charging ten cents a cup. But that was only half the regular price, and Joker threw in the Dixie Cup for nothing.

He was not lacking for customers this evening——George and Robert stood waiting their turn.

"What kind of chili are you going for?" asked Robert.

"I'm not much of a chili type of guy," said George. "But I'll look for something that doesn't seem too exotic."

"Why do you bother to come if you don't like chili?"

"It's for a good cause."

"That is true," said Robert. "The ladies raised over three

hundred dollars last year."

George whistled. "That's a lot of money."

"Yah, and it helps lots of folks. A lot of it's given to the families of miners who have suffered accidents or been killed. I saw you brought Myrtle. How's that relationship going?"

George leaned over close to the reverend. "I'm going to ask her to marry me."

"Very good!" said Robert. "Tonight?"

"No, next month—on Valentine's Day."

"Good luck."

"Mr. Mayor," said Joker, "a glass for you and the good reverend here?"

"Yah," said George, handing Joker two dimes. "And I'll pay for my friend's beer."

"Robert," said George as they walked away, beers in hand, "let's go someplace and talk. I want to pick your brain about streetlights."

"My. That does sound like a scintillating topic of conversation."

"What did you get?" asked Daisy as Myrtle returned to the table, a cup of chili in hand.

"Moose," said Myrtle, sliding into her seat.

"Huh," said Daisy. "I hope it isn't that moose you almost ran down when you first got to town."

Myrtle looked at the bowl. She had forgotten about that moose. She was driving down the road when the moose ambled out in front of her. She'd stopped the car just in time to avoid hitting the animal. After a five-minute standoff, she had enticed the moose to continue on its way with the help of two apples she'd picked up in Wisconsin. She sighed and pushed the bowl away from her.

"Not going to eat it?" asked Daisy.

Myrtle shook her head. "You just ruined my appetite for

moose."

"Pass it over here," said Daisy. "I'll take care of it for you."

"Myrtle," said Paige, "you remember last summer I told you I was writing a book?"

"Yes," said Myrtle. "How is that going?"

"Great! It's finished and I now have a publisher."

"Wonderful! I'm so happy for you. What is the book about?"

"It's a children's book—"

A loud crash followed by a cascade of swearing caused them all to turn and look in the direction of Joker and his beer stand where he and another man were involved in an altercation. The second man was waving a knife around.

Henri, along with three other men, hurried to break up the fight. He and one of the men grabbed the man with the knife. The other two restrained Joker.

Myrtle watched as Henri put the knife-wielder in an arm lock, disarmed him, and hurried him through the door and outside. Joker righted the table on which his Dixie Cups had been stacked and went back to dispensing beer.

"I'm going to go see what that was all about," said Myrtle.

Minutes later she returned. "It seems the man with the knife wanted a beer but didn't want to pay for it. Joker told him where he could go, and the man drew his knife and charged Joker, and knocked the table over. That was the crash we heard."

"Who was the man?" asked Daisy, already forming in her head the story for the next edition of the newspaper for which she was a reporter.

"George said he was Declan Murphy. He's not highly regarded around town, a real troublemaker. Okay, I'm going to try the rabbit. Anybody else want anything?"

CHAPTER FOUR

George had heard from a friend, Milton Applebee, a professor at the Michigan College of Mines in Houghton, that an extravaganza had been planned for Saturday night. He was driving over in his Briscoe automobile along with Myrtle, Daisy, and Eddie.

"Tell me again what this is we're going for," said Myrtle, as she snuggled deeper under the two blankets she had brought along.

The thermometer on the front porch of the boarding house had registered two degrees below zero when they left.

"The students are putting on a winter carnival," said George, not taking his eyes off the slippery, snow-covered road. "There'll be circus-style acts and bands and contests—speed skating and figure skating."

"Which one are you entered in?" asked Eddie from the back seat.

"Hah!" said George. "I wish. I'm afraid my skating days are behind me——except for nice, gentle laps around a rink or on a pond."

"Is this going to be indoors or outdoors?" asked Daisy.

"Because if it's outdoors, I'm staying in the car."

Myrtle twisted her head and looked at her. She was buried almost as deep under her blankets as Myrtle.

"Why, do you think it's warmer in here than outside?"

"There's an idea for you, George," said Eddie. "Invent someting dat will heat cars."

George nodded, still intent on the road. "It's indoors," he said, "at the Amphidrome."

"Is it heated?" asked Daisy. Her teeth began to chatter.

"It's an ice skating rink," said George. "I doubt they'll have a roaring fire going."

"Speaking of fire—who's watching the fire station tonight?" asked Myrtle.

"Robert," said Eddie. "He said he had his sermon all done for tomorrow so he had the time."

"How many people attend the Lutheran church?" asked Daisy. "Seems like everybody I know is Catholic."

"Most of the Finns who live around here are Lutheran," said George. "I think it's almost the state religion back in Finland."

"I'd like to go to a service there sometime," said Myrtle. "Reverend Albrecht is a very nice man, and I love Saija."

"I'll go with you," said Daisy.

Myrtle turned around again. "Okay, maybe tomorrow."

*****

As George slowed the car down, Myrtle and Daisy, mouths wide open, stared in disbelief at the giant structure that loomed before them.

"Wow!" exclaimed Daisy. "That looks like a castle!"

"That can't be the Amphi…Amphi…" Myrtle tried to get the word out.

"Amphidrome," said George. "No, that's an addition that

structure was built. It's used as a community ballroom. The armory is there, too."

"If that's the add-on," said Myrtle, "I can't wait to see what the main structure looks like."

"Oh, it's not as big as this part;" said George, "although it is pretty big."

He brought the car to a stop in front of a considerably smaller, but still impressive, building covered with a curved roof.

"Here's the Amphidrome," he said. "Everybody out."

"Well, *I* think it's pretty big," said Daisy.

"Wait 'til you see inside," said George.

CHAPTER FIVE

"Welcome to the circus," said the young man dressed up as a clown, as he greeted Myrtle and the others at the door.

"Circus?" said Daisy. "Will there be real animals?"

"Yes, indeed," said the clown. "Dogs like you've never seen before."

"Is that all?" asked Daisy, the disappointment evident on her face.

"Oh my, no," said the clown. "There will also be horses and elephants and a camel and . . . well, you'll just have to see for yourself. But you must hurry—the show is about to begin."

Daisy brightened. "Well, okay, then."

As they entered the main arena, George said, "Of course, Daisy, they won't be real animals; except perhaps for the dogs."

"What do you mean, 'they won't be real'?" asked Myrtle.

"As the young man said, you'll see."

The Amphidrome's interior was as impressive as the exterior. Rows of bleacher seats ran down both sides of the building, enough to seat several thousand people. Today, only the middle section on one side was filled with spectators—around six hundred, George estimated.

The four of them hurried to find their seats and had barely settled in when another young man dressed as a ringmaster skated out onto the ice.

"Ladies and gentlemen," his voice rang out as he removed his top hat and bowed to the crowd. "Welcome to our Winter Festival, featuring the best circus entertainment you shall ever find in all of Copper County."

A round of applause rang out.

"And now, for our first act—Peapicker and his wonder dog, Flea!"

Everybody watched as a gorgeous border collie dashed onto the ice, followed by another clown-clad young man who proceeded to put his charge through a series of tricks: jumping through and over hoops of varying sizes. For the finale, the clown told the dog to sit. Then he walked away from him about thirty yards, turned, raised his hand, held it for a split second, and lowered it. At the signal, Flea took off running for all his worth toward his master. As he got within about five yards, the man raised his arm again causing the dog to come to a sliding stop in a sitting position until he was mere inches away, whereupon, Peapicker picked him up and bowed to the applauding spectators.

"That was fun," said Myrtle as the ringmaster skated back out onto the ice.

For the next twenty minutes, they watched as students dressed in animal costumes—the horses, elephants, and camel the young man at the door had promised Daisy—went through various skits.

"Hope you're satisfied," Eddie leaned over and whispered to Daisy.

"Oh, they're funny all right," she replied. "But they ain't

real."

Following the animals, came a 'strong man' dressed in animal skin who first bent a—supposedly—iron bar into a horseshoe shape, then bent it back; a juggler displaying his skill with a variety of items, the last being three lighted torches; and a young woman who walked twenty-five yards on a tightrope strung twelve feet off the ground.

"Ladies and gentlemen," said the ringmaster again skating onto the ice as the tightrope was being disassembled, "we will now have a twenty-minute intermission while the ice is being cleared. But stick around—the best is yet to come."

About a dozen men who had been sitting in the stands poured out onto the ice with shovels and began smoothing it from the previous acts.

"Do they have female students at the college?" Myrtle asked George.

"My friend said girls have been studying here for over thirty years."

"Really?" exclaimed Myrtle. "What kind of degree do they receive?"

"Oh, they don't get a degree."

Myrtle's brow furrowed. "They don't get a degree? Why not?"

"They just don't," said George. "The college only confers degrees on the men."

"That's unacceptable," said Myrtle. "Isn't there a law against that?"

"Apparently not; it's been going on for thirty years."

"Humph," said Myrtle. "I wouldn't waste my money—or time—going to college if I couldn't get a degree."

"So, what do you think is more important?" asked George. "Getting a degree or getting an education?"

Myrtle didn't say anything for a minute.

"Well, I don't think it's fair," she answered finally.

"I guess most of the girls are children of the professors or wealthy businessmen who live in the area. Maybe they don't need the degree because they'll just get married."

"Just quit talking, George," said Myrtle. "You're only making it worse."

"And now, ladies and gentlemen," said the ringmaster, who had returned to the center stage, "we have a number of students who fancy themselves expert skaters. We shall see just how expert they are. We shall have a flight of races which should show us who the fastest skater is. We have twelve contestants, Mr. Antonio Marchand, Mr...."

"George, I bet you was pretty fast in your day," said Eddie.

George smiled. "I daresay, I could have held my own against the likes of these."

"The first round of two laps around the rink will include Mr. Marchand, Mr. Higgins, Mr. Patja, and Mr. Kaalinpää," said the ringmaster.

Myrtle looked around the rink and saw that barrels had been set up at varying intervals.

"The first two finishers," continued the ringmaster, "will advance to the next round."

He turned and addressed the racers.

"Gentlemen, to your marks."

The four men lined up, bodies poised to leap forward.

"On your mark," said the ringmaster, "get set . . . go!"

Blades scraping, the four men set off. One racer—Myrtle thought she remembered he had been introduced as Mr. Patja—broke away into an early lead, but he was soon overcome by Mr. Higgins. Around the rink they flew, ice chips shooting up behind their skates. As they approached the finish line, it looked as though the winner would prevail by a slim margin.

Now everyone was on their feet, cheering on their favorite.

As the racers blazed across the finish line it was apparent that Mr. Higgins had held on by a hair. While the three remaining skaters congratulated him, the ringmaster introduced the next set of racers.

Another two rounds, each one with four of the remaining original twelve skaters, produced six finalists, the first and second finishers in each flight. Two rounds with three skaters each brought the contest to the finale: a race between Mr. Higgins and Mr. Jaakkola.

It was apparent who the favorite was between the Finns who filled the stands and almost everybody else, including Myrtle and her bunch.

This race was to be three times around the rink on ice pretty torn up by the prior contestants.

As in his previous races, Mr. Jaakkola broke fast and was off to a good lead. Slowly but surely Mr. Higgins began to gain on him until, just as they came around the far bend the last time, Mr. Higgins put on a burst of speed and rushed past the finish line less than two feet in front of his competitor.

A loud cry went up: a reverberation of victory from Mr. Higgins' backers and a yelp of disappointment from the rest.

But Mr. Jaakkola proved he was a good sport when he skated over to Mr. Higgins and grabbed him in a bear hug.

"Congratulations," he said as he let Mr. Higgins go. "Well done."

Everyone broke out in applause.

"And now," said the ringmaster, skating to the middle of the rink, "the grand finale. But first, there will be a fifteen minute intermission while our cleaning crew takes care of the ice."

"I'm going to get a breath of fresh air," said Myrtle. "Maybe look for a ladies' room."

"I'll come with you," said Daisy. "This has been fun," she

said, as she followed Myrtle out of the stands.

"It sure has," Myrtle replied. "I'm anxious to see what the grand finale is."

When they reached the ladies' room, they found a line extending out the door.

"I don't have to go that bad," said Daisy.

"Me neither," said Myrtle. "Let's step outside."

"My God, it's gotten colder," said Daisy as they stood shivering outside the door.

"At least it's not snowing much," said Myrtle.

"Let's go back in," said Daisy. "I'm freezing my tush off."

By the time they reached their seats, the young men with the shovels had finished their task and the ringmaster was ready to reveal the grand finale.

"Ladies and gentlemen; all the way from New York, I am excited to announce the presence of one of America's premier women figure skaters: Beatrix Loughran!"

The crowd began to whistle and shout and stomp their feet on the bleachers.

"I guess they all know who she is," said Daisy.

"*I* know who she is," said Myrtle. "I read about her in the *New York Times*. She's going to be competing at the U.S. figure skating championships in a few months. She is *really* good."

"Where do you get *dat* paper?" asked Eddie.

"It's one of the out-of-town newspapers we get at the library," answered Myrtle. "You should stop by sometime and see what else we have. Look, there she is!"

Beatrix, dressed in a long black skirt and wearing a fur jacket, a fur cap perched on her head, skated out into the middle of the arena, the applause increasing in intensity. It abruptly stopped when the first strains of Saint-Saën's "The Swan" from *The Carnival of the Animals* drifted over the ice from where a young man sat playing on an upright piano.

Myrtle watched, transfixed, as Beatrix glided through her motions, seemingly one with the music and the ice.

She executed her final turn and sank into a curtsy. Everyone rose to their feet, applauding and whistling, and then slowly began to disperse.

"Let's wait until the crowd thins out before we go," said George.

Minutes later, they were outside. It was snowing harder now.

"You know, George, it could be a little rough gettin' back tonight," said Eddie. "Why don't we get a couple rooms at da Douglas House? You and I could share one and da girls da other one."

"I don't think it's going to get that bad," replied George. "I'd prefer to go on home. What about you ladies?"

"I'd rather sleep in my own bed tonight if I had a choice," said Daisy.

"I'll go along with whatever you all decide," said Myrtle.

George thought for a minute. "Let's go home, then. I'm sure it will be okay. It's only twenty miles."

By the time they'd gotten out of town, the snow was coming down harder, and George was having trouble finding the road.

"George, I'm concerned," said Myrtle, squinting through the snow-splattered windshield in a vain attempt to see where they were.

"It's okay," said George. "We'll be fine."

He wasn't at all sure they would be, though.

Five miles further out, George felt the car start to slide to the right.

"George," cried Myrtle, "we're going off the road!"

"Hold on," he said as he tried in vain to regain control.

Within minutes they had plowed into a snow bank.

"Everybody okay?" asked George, turning around to check on Daisy and Eddie in the back seat.

"We're fine," said Eddie. "Nutting hurt."

George got out of the car and looked at the snow bank covering the front of the automobile.

"We're going to have to dig it out," he said. "I have a shovel tied to the back, Eddie, if you'd get it for me."

Eddie removed the shovel and walked around to the front of the car.

"Here," said George, "I'll do it."

"Nah," said Eddie. "Dat's what us Irish is made for, stuff like dis."

He started to shovel, snow flying to the side.

"I'm cold," said Daisy.

"I'm coming back there with you," said Myrtle, climbing into the back seat. "Maybe we can keep each other warm."

Thirty minutes of furious shoveling removed enough snow so that George thought they could push the car out.

"Myrtle, you steer. Eddie and I will push."

"Me, too," said Daisy, jumping out of the car. "I'll help."

Try as hard as they could, the car wouldn't budge. After twenty minutes, George said, "It's no good. We're stuck."

"I saw a light in a farmhouse 'bout a mile back," said Eddie. "Why don't I hike back dere and see if da guy's got some horses he can pull us out?"

"Okay," said George. "I'll stay here with the women."

Forty-five minutes later, he and Myrtle and Daisy watched as two horses——good sturdy Percherons——approached, pulling a farm wagon with Eddie and the farmer sitting on the bench.

"This here's Mr. Thornton," said Eddie, jumping down from the wagon. "He was kind enough to hitch up his horses and come down here. We'll be able to pull da car out wit dem. And if we can't, Mr. Thornton said he'd carry us on into Booker Falls and we could come back for da car tomorrow."

"That's kind of you, Mr. Thornton," said Myrtle.

"Okay," said Mr. Thornton, "let's git 'em hitched up and see what dey can do, eh?"

It took but a few minutes for the two horses, strong ropes running from their harnesses to the car, to dislodge it from what remained of the snowdrift and have it back on the road.

"Mr. Thornton," said George, taking several bills from his wallet and offering them to the farmer, "I can't thank you enough. You've been a lifesaver."

"Ah, no need for da money," said Mr. Thornton, waving his hand. "Dat's what neighbors are for out here, eh? Tell ya what. Next time you folks pass dis way in da spring stop at da farm. We got some of da best apple orchards around. I'll give you a good price for a bushel. Now, you git on home, and be careful."

"Well, thanks again," said George. "All right ladies, back in the car. Let's go home."

*****

A little after two in the morning, the Briscoe pulled up in front of the boarding house and two exhausted women straggled through the front door to find Mrs. Darling, Henri, and Pierre all waiting in the parlor.

"My lands!" cried Mrs. Darling. "Where you two been? We expected you back hours ago!"

Myrtle thankfully accepted the cup of hot apple cider Pierre offered her, then plopped down on the sofa and explained what had happened.

"But you're okay?" asked Mrs. Darling. "You din't get hurt?"

"No, Mrs. Darling," said Daisy, who was holding the cup

of apple cider Henri had brought her. "We're both fine; just tired and cold and ready for bed."

"I knew I shouldn't have let George drag you up there in this weather," said Henri. "I shouldn't have allowed you to go."

Myrtle thrust out her chin and looked at Henri.

"*Allowed* us to go? Mr. de la Cruz, no one *allows* us to do anything! We are twentieth century women——Daisy and I. We do what we like. I don't have to ask permission from you or anyone else. You are not my mother or my father or…or my husband. And even if you were, I do not have to ask for your permission."

"I just…I…I only…" stammered a chastened Henri.

Myrtle downed the rest of her drink in one swallow.

"Thank you for the hot cider, Mrs. Darling," she said, "and for your concern. I'm going to bed now."

Fifteen minutes later, she was snuggled under her covers, fast asleep. She hadn't even bothered to brush her teeth.

Sunday service at the Lutheran Church would have to wait another week.

CHAPTER SIX

In the two and a half years of living under the same roof, Daisy and Myrtle had become the closest of friends, each coming to regard the other as the sister she'd never had.

They didn't look alike: nearly six feet tall, Daisy towered over her housemate by a good six inches. Neither was beautiful in the ordinary sense. Daisy's face was plain but pleasant; Myrtle's had more of a pixyish quality. And while Daisy possessed a sturdy, almost athletic, build, Myrtle was slender, frail some would say.

One thing they had in common, however, was their fierce independence. Daisy's had been forged growing up on the south side of Chicago, the only child of a working-class single mom. She never knew who her father was.

Ten years ago she'd left, convinced she had killed her husband in a fight, only to discover later that he had survived, but then died in a construction accident. She'd changed her name from Gwen Farking and taken the one by which she was now known: Daisy O'Hearn.

Myrtle's self-reliance was shaped by two years of service as a telephone operator in France for the Allied Expeditionary

Force. Officially designated the Signal Corps Female Telephone Operators Unit, the women quickly became known to the GIs as the "Hello Girls" because, unlike the French operators who always answered "Bonjour," the American girls always greeted callers with "Hello."

She was born and grew up in New Orleans, the only child of a middle-class family. Her father worked for the city and her mother was a professional musician, one of the original violinists hired by the New Orleans Symphony Orchestra.

Tonight, Daisy was waiting in the parlor nursing a cup of Thimbleberry tea when Myrtle came through the front door a few minutes after ten o'clock. The status of Myrtle's love life was one of Daisy's obsessions.

"So, how was it?" she asked.

Myrtle had told her that Henri had invited her out to dinner for Valentine's Day. They were going to an Italian restaurant in Houghton where he had taken her once before.

It had been as she remembered it, she said. Each table was covered with a red and white checked tablecloth with a vase holding a single daisy next to a small lit candle. Even the violin player was the same little man who had serenaded them on their previous visit.

"Did you have the lamb again?" asked Daisy.

"No," said Myrtle. She removed her coat and dropped it on the sofa. "Stuffed eggplant."

"Oooh! Was it good?"

"Delicious. And it went down very easy with the wine."

"How much wine?"

"I stopped counting."

Myrtle eyed Daisy's cup. "Is the water still hot?"

"Should be. I only heated it a few minutes ago."

Myrtle jumped up and headed for the kitchen. While she was fixing her tea, Henri came through the door.

"Get the horse put away?" she asked.

Henri just grunted and passed on through the kitchen and up the stairs.

"Did I see Henri just pass by?" asked Daisy when Myrtle returned to the parlor. "He didn't even say hi."

"I suppose he's not in a very good mood," said Myrtle, settling down into the chair next to Daisy's.

"Why, what happened?"

"He asked me to marry him."

"What? He did? What did you say?"

"I told him the same thing I told George earlier today when he brought me lunch at the library."

"Wait a minute!" exclaimed Daisy, sitting up straight in the chair. "George asked you to marry him too? You got proposed to *twice* today?"

Myrtle nodded and sipped her tea.

"Well, what did you tell him—them?"

"That I wasn't ready."

"That you weren't ready to get married?"

Myrtle shook her head. "No, that I wasn't ready to say yes —to either of them."

"You get two proposals of marriage in the same day and you turn both of them down?" Daisy stared at Myrtle. "You're something else, you know it?"

Myrtle shrugged. "What can I say? Anyway, how did your dinner go with Eddie?"

"We had a great meal at the Hungry Hog. Not as elegant as yours, I'm sure, but I liked it."

Myrtle laughed. "The Hungry Hog. What a name for a restaurant."

"After the Juicy Pig burned down and they rebuilt it, I guess Mr. Treadwell wanted to give it a different name."

"He's the owner?"

"Yep."

"And I'm sure they're still serving everything porcine," said Myrtle.

"Yep—pork chops, pork loin, pork sausage, pork ribs, bacon, ham, hot dogs, pig snout—"

"And pickled pigs feet," added Myrtle.

"My favorite," said Daisy. "So, when *will* you be ready?"

"Ready for what?"

"To say yes—to getting married."

"You'll be the first to know," said Myrtle. "Okay, the third—there'll be me and whoever the lucky guy is, then you."

"Okay, now the suspense is killing me," said Daisy.

CHAPTER SEVEN

The library was as quiet as the frozen, snow-covered pond outside Myrtle's office window. Even the boiler had ceased its banging since Roger Lampley, owner of the Roger Dodger Plumbing Company, had come two weeks earlier and bled the air that was causing such a ruckus.

Less than a dozen students had ventured out from their dorm rooms into the frigid temperature that had wrapped itself around the whole area for the past month. Myrtle wondered why she should have kept the library open but decided that if even one person wanted to use it, that was sufficient reason to do so.

She stared through the window at a six-point buck on the far side of the pond as he casually nibbled the leaves of a red maple tree. Her hands were buried deep in the pockets of her cucumber-colored cardigan.

I should be working, she thought, *instead of standing here daydreaming*.

She had decided this was the week to catalog some of the books stored in the vault, a large chamber set underground below the library's main floor. The problem was that the room was not heated and, though it maintained a steady year-round temperature in the high fifties, during the winter it felt more like the forties.

Myrtle balled up her fists and dug deeper into her pockets.

"Myrtle?"

Myrtle turned to find Lydia Plummer at the door. Lydia was Myrtle's assistant, having taken her place when she was appointed head librarian last year after the death of her predecessor.

"Yes?" said Myrtle.

"There's a Professor Thatcher out here. He wants to know if we have some book on beekeeping. I can't find it in our card catalog."

"Let's go see what we can do," said Myrtle.

In his early seventies, Professor Edwin Thatcher still cut an impressive figure in a raccoon fur coat that came down to just below the top of his boots. Tufts of gray hair stuck out from beneath the chook atop his head. Pince-nez eyeglasses perched on a nose under which grew a magnificent walrus mustache. A pair of kidskin gloves covered his hands.

"Professor Thatcher, I'm Myrtle Tully, head librarian. What can I do for you?"

Professor Thatcher gave a slight bow. "Miss Tully, I am happy to make your acquaintance. I am looking for a book, not a new one, but one about seventy years old. It is titled *Da Hive and da Honey-bee* and was written by Lorenzo Langstroth. Is dere any chance you might have a copy of it in da library?"

"Mmm, I doubt it," said Myrtle. "I can look, but it may take some time. Do you have a telephone that I might contact you on if I come across it?"

"Certainly. Miss Maribel knows me well. She can connect us."

"The telephone operator?" said Myrtle.

"Yes, dat is she."

"Then I will let you know one way or the other. And if I find we do not have a copy I will contact the state library in Lansing. If anyone has one, it would be them. Are you interested in beekeeping Professor?"

Professor Thatcher's eyes lit up. The opportunity to talk with someone about beekeeping was always welcome.

"I am. And you?"

"The gardener who tended my parents' grounds in New Orleans was a beekeeper. He showed me his hives once. I wouldn't go near them. I was afraid they'd bite me."

"Technically, bees do not bite—dey sting. And, I admit, it can sometimes be painful—fatal, even."

"Have you ever been bit…stung, Professor?" asked Myrtle.

"Oh, my, yes—many times. I am fortunate I am not allergic to deir venom."

"Isn't it too cold here in the Upper Peninsula to have bees?"

"Dey do fine from late spring to early fall. In da winter I move da hives inside to keep dem warm. Do you enjoy honey, Miss Tully?"

"I love honey," said Myrtle. "Mrs. Darling has it out almost every meal."

"You reside at Mrs. Darling's boarding house?"

"I do. Do you know Mrs. Darling?"

"We are old acquaintances. And do you like candles?"

"I love candles, too!" exclaimed Myrtle. "Sometimes I almost wish I lived in a time before there was electricity."

"Trust me," said Professor Thatcher, "you do not. I grew up at a time when our sole source of light was by candlelight or oil lamps. Today is much better. You must come by my workshop sometime and I will show you how I make honey and candles."

"I would love that," said Myrtle. "What do you teach at the college, Professor?"

"I teach writing and penmanship."

"Are you an author?"

"I fear not. I lack da prerequisite imagination to put anything of interest to paper."

"As I said, I shall contact you when I have some word about the book you are looking for. And I shall look forward to visiting your workshop."

*****

The Salle de Spectacle Theater, located on Main Street right next to Reynolds Funeral Home, was the realization of a dream come true when Chase Irwin moved to the burgeoning town of Booker Falls, Michigan in 1899.

For ten years, Chase and his wife, who went by the stage name of Katch, performed a comedy act in vaudeville shows throughout New England. When Katch caught a cold that developed into pneumonia, resulting in her death, Chase was devastated.

Rather than continuing to perform on his own, he decided to head west and build a theater where vaudeville touring acts could perform. Over the years the Salle de Spectacle Theater also became a venue for plays.

It was one of these to which Myrtle had invited Henri to accompany her this evening.

"What's the name of this again?" asked Henri.

"*The Sleeping Car*," said Myrtle, as they settled into their seats.

"A car that sleeps?" said Henri. "That sounds ridiculous."

"No, it's a sleeping car on a train. The action takes place on a train."

"Is it a mystery?"

"No, a comedy. You'll enjoy it."

"Well, I'm sure I'll like the popcorn," said Henri, stuffing a handful into his mouth.

*****

When the final curtain came down, Henri found himself standing and applauding with gusto along with the other patrons.

"So, what do you think?" asked Myrtle as they exited out into the cold night.

"You were right," said Henri. "I did enjoy it. It was funny."

"I noticed you laughed the loudest when Aunt Mary was on stage."

"She was hilarious. That may have been the best acting I've ever seen."

"Let's have a drink," said Myrtle.

"You mean, invade Mrs. Darling's secret stash of sherry when we get back to the boarding house?"

"No. Why don't we go to Joker's?"

Henri stopped in his tracks and looked at Myrtle. "Joker's? That's . . . well, that's not exactly a place for ladies."

"I promise—tonight I won't act like a lady."

Henri laughed. "Okay, then, if you're up for it, so am I."

CHAPTER EIGHT

Myrtle looked forward to the annual St. Patrick's Day party at the fire station. She recalled how much fun she'd had last year when she and Daisy got to slide down the pole.

Then she had debated whether to ask George or Henri to accompany her. They both had standing invitations to attend, Henri as the county constable and George as the mayor. She'd finally settled on George—she wasn't quite sure why. But they'd had so much fun she decided to ask George again this year.

He jumped at the chance.

Her decision aside, Myrtle was a little surprised Henri hadn't asked her to go with him. He hadn't attended last year's celebration.

George, unlike Myrtle, Henri, and Daisy, was a native of Booker Falls. Other than three years at Rensselaer Polytechnic Institute in Troy, New York, he had lived his whole life here in his family home located in the town's finest neighborhood. Since 1914 he had served as mayor.

George had it all; six-foot-two, two hundred and ten pounds, he boasted an athletic build developed from playing amateur hockey. With hair the color of wheat and turquoise eyes, Myrtle thought him more handsome than Henri, who was not hard to look at either.

And, he was rich, thanks to a substantial inheritance, the result of his father's involvement in the early days of the area's lumber industry.

Tonight, when Myrtle walked through the front door of the fire station on George's arm, the answer to why Henri hadn't invited her became obvious: he was holding hands with Jessica Parker, a young, attractive black woman whom Myrtle remembered as the former housekeeper for Rudolph and Margaret Folger before the former was murdered and the latter moved back to her home in Mohawk.

Jessica was one of a handful of Negroes who called Booker Falls home including Henri, whose mother was white and father black.

It was Jessica who came to the door last year when Myrtle accompanied Henri to the Folger home to question Mrs. Folger about the death of her husband. Myrtle thought at the time she detected a spark between them.

Stately, nearly as tall as Henri, Jessica wore a white silk, sleeveless pullover dress with a scoop that accentuated her long, slender neck. The dropped-waist skirt featured two tiers of fringe. A silver sequined headband with a tuft of white feathers contrasted with her jet-black, bobbed hair. Skin the color of burnt sienna, Jessica was strikingly beautiful. The most amazing thing about the woman, though, was her sea-green eyes.

Myrtle was wearing the same green plaid slacks she'd worn when she first arrived in Booker Falls, along with her matching newsboy cap. At least the blouse was different: white, long-sleeved, made of cotton.

As much as she didn't want to admit it, Myrtle felt a spark

of jealousy.

"Hey, dere you two are," said Eddie, hurrying over to her and George, offering them the beers he was holding.

Prohibition might be the law of the land, but the normally law-abiding citizens of Booker Falls were not about to let that small technicality deter them from having fun.

"Ya decided to give it another whirl dis year, did ya?" asked Eddie.

"I had so much fun last year I couldn't resist," said Myrtle.

"Ya slidin' down da pole again?"

Myrtle giggled. She remembered her trepidation last year at sliding down the metal pole that extended from the second floor down to the first. She'd ended up doing it three times.

"I just might," she said. "Where's Daisy?"

Eddie pointed to where six couples were dancing to the music of a five-piece band.

"She latched on to Gus and she's got him doin' someting called da Turkey Trot."

Myrtle looked to where Eddie was pointing. Sure enough, there were Daisy and Gus, doing little jumps like a turkey. Myrtle rolled her eyes.

"Come on, George," she said, "let's find a table."

"There are some empty chairs where Henri and Jessica are sitting," he said.

"I don't think so," said Myrtle. "Oh, look, there's Saija. I so enjoyed her last year. Come on."

She grabbed George by the arm and began to lead him over to Saija's table.

George pulled up. "I'm pretty sure I'm capable of making it on my own."

"Oh, I'm sorry," said Myrtle, flustered. "I didn't mean…"

"It's okay. Come on, let's go. I have something I want to talk to Robert about anyway."

"Myrtle, I'm so happy to see you," gushed Saija, jumping up from her seat and embracing Myrtle while Robert stood and shook hands with George.

"I wouldn't miss it for anything," said Myrtle.

"Robert, I have something I'd like to discuss with you," said George.

Robert looked concerned. "Serious?" he asked.

George shook his head. "No, just what we talked about some time ago: new street lights."

Once the two men departed, Saija turned to Myrtle.

"So, are you and George…you know?"

"Seeing one another?"

Saija nodded. "He's one of the few eligible bachelors in town."

Myrtle smiled. "No, we're merely friends."

"Uh, huh—that's not what I hear."

"What—"

"Myrtle—about time you got here!"

Myrtle felt Daisy's ample arms surround her from the back.

"I see you didn't wait for me to get started having fun," said Myrtle, turning and giving her housemate a kiss on the cheek.

"Life is too short to wait around," said Daisy. "Where's George?"

"Off talking business with my husband," said Saija. "I'm going to go get us some drinks. Have a seat, Daisy."

"This isn't the same band as last year, is it?" asked Myrtle.

"No," said Daisy as she plopped down next to Myrtle. "They're called The Coppers."

"Are they policemen?"

"No, they work in the copper mines by day and play music at night."

"Where'd you learn to do the Turkey Trot?" asked Myrtle.

"Gus taught me. He said he picked it up in Detroit when he was there last month."

"You going to get Eddie to do it with you?"

Daisy's laugh could be heard all through the building.

"Are you kidding? Eddie's a great guy and I love him but one thing he's not is a dancer. What do you think of Henri's date?"

Myrtle's eyes shifted to the dance floor where Henri and Jessica twirled around doing the foxtrot.

"She's cute," said Myrtle.

"Cute? Are you kidding? She's a knockout! And I see you got all dressed up for the occasion."

Myrtle was beginning to feel shabbier by the minute.

"Okay, here we are," said Saija, returning to the table holding a tray with three glasses. "I assumed everyone wanted beer."

"Boy, I do," said Daisy, grabbing one of the glasses and putting it to her lips. "Mmm."

"Don't they have anything stronger?" asked Myrtle.

Saija and Daisy both looked at her.

"Why? Do you need something stronger?" asked Daisy.

"Never mind," said Myrtle. She got up from her chair. "I'm going to go powder my nose."

"I'll go with you," said Saija.

"No need," said Myrtle as she scurried off.

Fortunately, when Myrtle reached the bathroom, it was unoccupied. She rushed in, locked the door, then looked at herself in the cracked mirror.

She didn't even have any lipstick on.

"You're a mess," she said out loud.

A knock at the door made her straighten up.

"Occupied," she said.

"It's Daisy," came the voice from the other side of the door.

Myrtle unlocked the door and Daisy entered. Myrtle quickly locked the door again.

"What's going on?" asked Daisy.

"Look at me," said Myrtle. "I'm a mess."

Daisy stared at her without saying anything for a minute.

"You're right—you could use some help."

Myrtle burst into tears.

"Okay, okay," said Daisy. "It ain't that bad; nothing that can't be fixed. Now, you stay here—don't let anyone in 'til I get back."

"What if someone needs to use the bathroom?"

"Tell them you're doing them a favor by not letting them come in right away."

Myrtle nodded.

Minutes later Daisy returned with Saija.

"Daisy says you need some help," said Saija. "First, let's replace those tears on your face with some makeup."

"And then some lipstick," said Daisy.

"And then some lipstick," repeated Saija.

"And lose the cap," said Daisy.

"Yes, definitely," said Saija. "Unless you're planning on taking on a second job hawking newspapers on the corner, lose the cap."

Fifteen minutes later, after having fended off several irate would-be bathroom users, the three women emerged and returned to their table where George and Robert were waiting.

Myrtle thought she saw George's eyebrows lift—in approval, she hoped?

"Where have you three been?" asked Robert.

"We had some business to attend to," said Saija. "We don't ask where you and George disappear off to, do we?"

A shout rose above the noise in the room.

"Henri, you better come quick!"

They all looked to see who had summoned Henri.

Pete Simpson, one of the volunteer firemen, was at the front door, frantically waving his arms. "Henri—quick!"

Henri jumped up and followed Pete as he ran out the door, the rest of the crowd close on their heels.

Outside, Pete stopped and pointed at four men across the street in front of the Walther Building.

One man lay on the ground, while a second man stood brandishing a knife, attempting to fend off blows from a third man, who was wielding a cane.

Myrtle thought the man with the knife looked familiar.

The fourth man, Simon Abramovitz, owner of the town pawnshop, stood off to one side.

Henri raced across the street and caught the third man's arm just before his cane came down again on the second man.

"Hold it!" shouted Henri.

He moved between the two men and turned to the man with the knife.

"First of all, give me the knife."

"Who da hell are you?" asked the man, making no move to hand over his weapon.

Henri recognized him as Declan Murphy.

"You remember me," said Henri. "I arrested you at the Chili-Cook Off. Now, hand over your knife."

Grumbling unintelligibly, Declan handed Henri his knife.

"Now, what's going on here?" asked Henri.

"Dis old bastard's tryin' ta beat me ta death," said Declan. His face was contorted in anger.

The third man still lay on the ground, not speaking.

"He was kicking dat man," said the man with the cane. "I stopped him."

Henri looked at the man on the ground. He knew him. He was an Indian, who went by the single name of Grissom. Henri had seen him in town before. He'd never caused any trouble.

"It's true, Henri," said Simon. "He vas kicking dat poor Indian."

"Is that true? You were kicking this man?" asked Henri.

"What if I was?" said Declan. "He's a dirty Indian. Shouldn't even be on da street, anyway."

"Turn around. You're under arrest."

"Under arrest? For what?"

"Assault and battery."

"Assault and battery? On who? Dis old geezer was 'saultin' *me!*"

"Grissom," said Henri, nodding toward the Indian. He grabbed Declan, spun him around and started to reach for his handcuffs then realized he hadn't brought them. Why would he—he was going to a party.

"And you," said Henri, addressing the man with the cane. "What's your name?"

"This is Professor Thatcher," said Myrtle who by now had joined the group. "Professor Thatcher teaches at the college. He comes to the library sometimes."

"*Were* you trying to beat this man to death?" asked Henri.

"Not quite, sir; merely within an inch of his life," said a smiling Professor Thatcher.

Everyone who came out to see what was happening laughed.

"What are you goin' to do wit me?" asked Declan.

"Why, you're going to spend the night in jail. And tomorrow morning we'll see what Judge Hurstbourne has to say."

"Jail?" exclaimed Declan. "For kickin' a dirty Indian?"

"Why don't you try resisting arrest and we'll see if we can add another charge," said Henri. "Now, get moving. Myrtle, can you see if Grissom needs any assistance?"

"Wait!" said Declan. "Ain't you gonna arrest dat old geezer too?"

"For what?" asked Henri.

"For 'saultin' me. I was da one gettin' 'saulted."

"No," said Henri. "I reckon he might even get a medal."

Declan turned and glowered at Thatcher. "I'll get you, old man. I'll get you."

Myrtle had gone to see if Grissom needed any assistance, but he waved her off.

"I'm okay, Miss."

"Okay, folks, show's over," said Eddie. "Let's get back in da station and party. Perfessor, why don't you join us?"

"Why, I don't—"

"Yes, you do," said George, taking Thatcher by the elbow. "We're going to go in and celebrate."

"Celebrate what?" asked Thatcher.

"An honorable and upstanding citizen," said George.

CHAPTER NINE

"Myrtle, dear."

Myrtle rolled over and eyed the clock on the nightstand next to her bed.

"It can't be six o'clock already," she moaned. She rolled back over and shut her eyes.

"Myrtle, dear," came the voice again.

Myrtle knew that voice: it was Mrs. Darling's. And she knew what Mrs. Darling wanted. Myrtle had promised to go with her to the 8:30 mass at St. Barbara's. Her landlady was not a committed churchgoer but for some reason she wanted to be there this morning.

Normally, Myrtle wouldn't have minded. But yesterday—following the party at the fire station the night before——had been a hard one. Myrtle was painfully aware she'd had too much beer to drink.

"Yes, Mrs. Darling, I'm up," said Myrtle, struggling to get her feet out from under the covers.

Thirty minutes later, she made her way down to the dining room just as the grandfather clock in the corner of the room gave out a loud *bong*.

During her first year at the boarding house, Myrtle jumped every time the clock rang out, which it did every fifteen minutes. Now, she was used to it and even looked forward to it.

When it stopped working several years back—precisely at the moment of Mr. Pfrommer's death, it had been calculated —it was thought to be beyond repair. It was an eight-day clock and it had been Mr. Pfrommer who wound it once a week to keep it running. Henri took over the task after Mr. Pfrommer went to prison. When the clock died, Mrs. Darling called a watchmaker from Houghton who drove down and brought it back to life.

Henri and Pierre were already seated at the breakfast table. Both jumped up when Myrtle entered the room, but it was Henri who got to her chair first to pull it back for her.

"Good morning, Miss Tully," said Pierre.

"Mr. Longet," said Myrtle. She never had figured out why he continued to refer to her as 'Miss Tully' and not Myrtle. Then again, she still referred to him as 'Mr. Longet.'

"Let's hurry and eat," said Mrs. Darling, setting down two big bowls——one filled with biscuits, the other with sausage gravy. "Da eggs and pancakes will be right out. I don't want to be late to church. Oh, my . . . coffee—I forgot da coffee."

She scurried off to the kitchen.

"You're going to church this morning with Mrs. Darling?" said Pierre.

"Yes, but I don't know why," said Myrtle, as she ladled gravy over the biscuit she'd carefully arranged on her plate. "She doesn't usually want to go to church. I don't much want to myself today."

"Has it been a hard weekend?" asked Henri, smiling. He knew how much beer she'd consumed at the party.

"It's been a nice weekend," said Myrtle. *At least Friday*

night was; yesterday—not so much.

Mrs. Darling had returned by now with the coffee.

Myrtle moved her cup to allow her to fill it.

"Thank you, Mrs. Darling," she said. She looked at Daisy's empty chair. "Where's Daisy?"

"Poor girl said she was sleeping in," said Mrs. Darling, setting down a huge platter of pancakes and a pitcher of maple syrup. "Said she had a busy weekend."

Yeah, me, too, thought Myrtle. *Yet here I am.*

Myrtle only half-listened as Henri and Pierre discussed the latest goings-on at the legislature in Lansing. When the clock sounded out, warning it was fifteen minutes 'til eight, she excused herself, got up, and retreated upstairs to brush her teeth and comb her hair. When she came back downstairs, Mrs. Darling was waiting at the door.

"Henri said he'd take us in da sleigh," said Mrs. Darling, "but I told him I'd just as soon walk since it's so nice out."

Myrtle looked through the window of the front door. The ground was covered by at least three feet of snow and it was still coming down. She looked at the thermometer on the front porch, painted with the words, "Love's Temperature" and a picture of a man and woman in an embrace. The indicator had not yet reached double digits.

"Are you sure?" she asked.

"Oh, yah, sure. Come on, let's go."

*****

Forty-five minutes later, Myrtle breathed a sigh of relief when they reached the front door of the church. She removed her snowshoes, stacked them with the dozens of pairs already there, and followed Mrs. Darling into the sanctuary.

As Myrtle waited for the service to begin, she studied the eight stained-glass windows——four on each side of the sanctuary. A few years ago, Father Fabian had explained the significance of each of them to Myrtle, how they represented the primary events in the life of St. Barbara.

Myrtle liked Father Fabian. He was both friendly and funny. And he gave good sermons.

She fondled the rosary he'd given her once when she told him she had lost hers. It was a used one left to the church by a deceased member of the congregation. Made of beads of white pine, it held a medallion showing the standing figure of St. Barbara in a gown, a halo around her head. Myrtle smiled at the red specks that covered the beads, remembering Father Fabian telling her that originally the beads had been solid red but had been rubbed clean over time by the parishioner, Mrs. Rumbaugh.

The thought that the rosary had at one time brought comfort to someone else made it more special than if it were new.

*****

Following the service, Myrtle and Mrs. Darling lingered outside the church, greeting people. Having been a resident of Booker Falls her whole life, Mrs. Darling was friends with nearly everyone in town. Since she rarely attended church, everyone who exited the building stopped to say hello and inquire about her health.

To Myrtle's surprise, a great many of them also stopped to chat with her. She hadn't realized how well known she had become both because of her position at the college library—which was also available to the whole town—and her exploits solving murders over the past three years.

When the last of the well-wishers departed, Myrtle asked, "Ready to head home?"

"Nah," said Mrs. Darling. "I left fixins for sandwiches in da kitchen and told da boys and Daisy dey could help demselves to it, and whatever else dey found. I'm plannin' on eatin' out for a change."

Myrtle looked at her landlady in surprise. She never missed lunch at the boarding house except on special days such as the Fourth of July or when the two of them drove to Marquette to visit Mr. Pfrommer in prison.

"Well, okay, then," she said. "Madeline's?"

"Yah, it's too far to walk to da Hungry Hog. But sometime I want to try it—see if dere cookin' is as good as mine."

"That would be impossible," said Myrtle, smiling.

Most towns the size of Booker Falls had more than two establishments that served food. But, as a large number of the population consisted of miners who took their lunches with them to the mines every day, the demand for restaurants here was not great. In addition, every miner's breakfast and most evening meals were shared at home with their families.

Ice cream treats—sundaes, banana splits, milkshakes, ice cream in bowls or cones—and hot dogs were available at the Polar Bear.

But on those rare occasions when the miners and other working men ate out, their restaurant of choice was the Hungry Hog, the successor to the Juicy Pig, where portions were generous and prices affordable.

Not to say Miss Madeline's was expensive; it just had a nicer ambience than the Hungry Hog, slightly higher prices, and a more extensive and varied menu—meaning not as much emphasis on food of a porcine nature.

Predating The Polar Bear next door by one year, the restaurant had its beginning in 1848 when John Ackerson, his forty-year-old wife, Madeline, and their two children who still lived at home moved from West Virginia to the newly established town of Booker Falls. John had taken a position with the recently formed Quincy Mining Company which had just dug its first shaft in a hillside above Portage Lake.

Madeline had been a cook for a restaurant in their previous location. With this move, she decided she no longer wanted to work for someone else. Pitching a tent in a vacant lot on the main street, she began serving soup and something she never heard of in West Virginia—pasties, a local favorite made of meat and vegetables baked in a pastry.

Within two years, business expanded to the point where an actual building was constructed. Now it held a large dining room with two dozen round tables covered with white tablecloths——some seating two customers, some four and, in the back two corners, larger ones where as many as eight people could gather.

In the middle of the fifteen-foot-high ceiling hung a Sophia thirty-five-light candle-styled, tiered chandelier that, about a quarter of a century earlier, had replaced the original chandelier that required real candles.

A half-dozen Metropolitan chandeliers placed around the ceiling provided additional light.

Photographs of people and town buildings from over the past three decades adorned the walls. A stuffed moose head mounted over the front door held court. And on one wall a fireplace six feet wide provided cozy warmth to augment the heat provided by the boiler in the basement.

Myrtle's favorite waitress was Mona, one of Madeline's grandchildren. Mona waited on Myrtle the first time she ate at Miss Madeline's with Daisy. At that time Mona was eighteen. Now she was twenty-one and a mother.

"Miss Myrtle, what'll it be today? Corn chowder? Meatloaf? Fried chicken?"

"Something hot—" said Myrtle, "very hot."

"Dat would be our tree-meat surprise chili," said Mona.

"Tree-meat?" asked Mrs. Darling. "What are da tree meats?"

"Beef and chicken," said Mona.

"That's two," said Myrtle. "What's the third?"

"Dat's da surprise, eh?" said Mona, a big grin stretching across her face.

"Surprise, huh?" said Myrtle. "Okay, I'm on—bring me the three-meat surprise chili."

"How 'bout you, Mrs. Darling?" asked Mona. "Wanna give it a try?"

"I tink a bowl of plain old chicken noodle soup will work fine for me," Mrs. Darling replied.

"Oh, look, Mrs. Darling," said Myrtle, "there's Professor Thatcher."

Mrs. Darling turned to look. "Yah, you're right, dat is him. What a distinguished-looking gentleman—so tragic."

"Tragic?"

"What happened 'tween him and his brudder—and his brudder's wife. Da whole affair."

Myrtle frowned. "He had an affair with his brother's wife?" she whispered.

"Oh, no, nudding like dat."

"What was it then?"

"Back when da Thatcher boys was young, Edwin, da older one, was datin' Caroline Thornapple. Den he went off to college. When he come back home for Christmas he found out Caroline had up and married Orville and she was pregnant. Word is, Edwin went crazy; accused Orville of stealin' Caroline out from under him, broke tings, threatened Orville. Dey never was close after dat. Den da accident happened. Dat was da icing on da cake."

"The accident?"

"Da carriage accident—ten years ago."

"Oh, right," said Myrtle. "I remember Henri telling me you told him Orville's wife was killed in a carriage accident."

"Dat's right. Orville was drivin' da carriage and he was drunk. He admitted it to Constable Barnoble, said he was drivin' too fast, too, and lost control. Dat got Edwin even madder at Orville. I don't tink Edwin ever got over Caroline."

"He never married?"

"Nah, never did—good lookin' man like him—what a waste."

"Ah, here's our food," said Myrtle as Mona set the bowls down on the table.

*****

"That was delicious," said Myrtle, placing her soup spoon down on the plate under her bowl. "How was your chicken noodle soup, Mrs. Darling?"

"Very tasty," said Mrs. Darling, dabbing her lips with her napkin. She leaned across the table. "But not as good as mine."

Myrtle laughed. "No, I wouldn't think so."

They paid their bill and exited onto Main Street. The snow was still coming down.

"Oh, oh," said Myrtle. "This doesn't look good."

"Da snow?"

"No, that," said Myrtle, pointing across the street.

They watched as Professor Thatcher neared the corner of a building around which another man was approaching. Myrtle recognized him from the night of the St. Patrick's Day party: Declan Murphy.

As the two men collided, Professor Thatcher was knocked to the ground.

"You crazy old man!" shouted Murphy. "Why don't you watch where you're goin'. Wait—you dat old geezer what hit me wit a cane, ain't ya?"

Murphy pulled a knife from his belt.

"I should of taken care of you den," he said, stepping closer to Edwin, who lay sprawled on the ground.

"You don't want to do that."

Murphy stopped and turned around. Myrtle held her two-shot derringer pointed straight at him.

Murphy laughed. "This ain't none o' your business, Missy. 'Sides, you probly don't even know how to use dat little gun."

"Are you willing to find out?" asked Myrtle.

"Go away," said Murphy. He turned back to Edwin and started to kneel, the knife pointed at the elderly man on the ground. He stopped when he heard the retort of the derringer and saw the snow fly up next to his boot. He looked at Myrtle, fire in his eyes.

"Why, you—"

"I have one more shot here," said Myrtle. "I won't be aiming at the snow the next time."

Murphy slowly got to his feet.

Myrtle was shaking inside. But the calmness she managed in her voice told Murphy she wasn't kidding. He also wasn't sure he wanted to test her accuracy. He slid the knife back into his belt.

"Next time," he said, backing away. He looked down at Edwin. "Next time for you, too."

Then he walked off.

Myrtle slipped the derringer back into her purse and hurried to help Edwin up off the ground.

"Professor, are you all right?" she asked.

"Thanks to you, Miss Tully." He reached down, picked up the chook that had fallen off when he was knocked down, and placed it back on his head. "Thanks to you."

"That man is dangerous," said Myrtle. "You'd best avoid him if at all possible."

"I shall," said Edwin. "And you likewise—you stay clear of him, too."

*****

Henri was furious when Myrtle and Mrs. Darling returned to the boarding house and told him what had happened. He'd rushed out to look for Murphy to arrest him and charge him with assault.

Three hours later he returned, still seething with anger.

Murphy was nowhere to be found.

CHAPTER TEN

Myrtle viewed Saturdays with mixed emotions.

On the one hand, it meant the end of her workweek. Tomorrow, Sunday, would be her one day off. On the other hand, Saturday was Lydia's day off, which meant all the work was on Myrtle's shoulders today.

She had finished restocking the books that had come in the day before and returned to the front desk when Professor Thatcher came through the front door, ushering in a blast of cold air.

Myrtle smiled as he approached her. She liked the professor. He was friendly, refined and, as far as she could determine, highly intelligent——a real gentleman to boot.

"Professor Thatcher," said Myrtle, "it's so nice to see you today. What has brought you out in this terrible weather?"

Edwin doffed his hat. "Miss Tully, you are a ray of sunshine in an otherwise dismal day. I have come to pick up a book Miss Plummer set aside for me yesterday when I called: *Lessons on the Human Body* by Orestes M. Brands."

"Ah, let me look," said Myrtle, ducking her head under the desk.

Seconds later, she reappeared, book in hand.

"Here it is, just waiting for you."

"Ah, yes," said Edwin picking up the book. "This is exactly what I'm looking for. And here;" he reached into the brown paper sack he held in his hand, pulled out a candle, and laid it on the desk, "this is for you."

"Oh, my, it's beautiful," said Myrtle. "Did you make this? It's beeswax, isn't it?"

"I did, and it is."

"I can't help but admire your gloves," said Myrtle. "I'm considering getting a pair myself."

"Yah, dey're kidskin. I always wear gloves, sometimes even in da summer. I almost feel naked if I don't have a pair on. Miss Tully, I was hoping you might be able to come by my workshop dis evening. I want to show you how I make my candles and I also have some honey to give you, which I forgot to bring."

"Tonight?" said Myrtle. She was looking forward to a quiet evening at the boarding house. "Would tomorrow be all right? I don't have to work tomorrow."

"Tonight would be better, eh?" said Edwin. "I would very much appreciate it if it's at all possible."

How can I refuse? wondered Myrtle.

"Of course," she said. "The library closes at six. I'll come directly from here."

Edwin beamed. "Good! I shall expect you den. Good day, Miss Tully."

He doffed his hat, turned, and left.

*****

Myrtle had arranged a compromise over the winter between George and Henri, both of whom wanted to pick her up at the library after work each day and drive her home. It was too cold and the snow was too deep for her to make the two-mile walk in the dark, they'd said.

Independent as she was, Myrtle remembered her first winter in Booker Falls when she'd broken a strap on one of her snowshoes and gotten lost in a blizzard on her way home from the college. Had it not been for Henri and Daisy, she would have frozen to death.

She didn't want to hurt either of the men's feelings so she had agreed George could pick her up on Mondays, Wednesdays, and Fridays, while Henri's days would be Tuesdays, Thursdays, and Saturdays.

By the end of March, however, closing time at the library had long preceded sunset and while several feet of snow covered the ground, the temperature was no longer a factor. Nevertheless, she had allowed each of them to continue his routine as she knew it made them feel useful.

Besides, she enjoyed their company.

Today was Saturday, so it was Henri who was waiting for her at six o'clock when she exited the library. Myrtle was surprised to see he had brought his car and not the sleigh.

He didn't bother to get out or open the door. He had learned long ago Myrtle neither expected nor required such assistance, that she was, she said, perfectly capable of accomplishing the feat by herself.

When she first arrived in Booker Falls, her Model N was the first automobile ever owned by anyone in town, though others had passed through on their way to somewhere else.

Later, George had followed suit by going all the way to Jackson to purchase a robin's-egg blue Briscoe Touring Car, four-door with a convertible top, leather-covered seats, headlights, and a horn.

Not to be outdone, Henri, in spite of his dislike of "horseless carriages" had, within a year, joined the small group of automobile owners. His car, in which he was waiting for Myrtle this evening, was a Packard Town Car with a twelve-inch-high bell attached to the hood. A chain ran from the bell to a lever next to the steering wheel so Henri could ring the bell when he was in a hurry and needed people, horses, carriages, sleds, and other automobiles to move out of the way.

Now, several dozen automobiles called Booker Falls home.

"I was looking forward to a sleigh ride," said Myrtle as she settled into the seat next to Henri.

"Time to start driving this," said Henri. "The streets and roads are in pretty good shape now."

"Okay, then," said Myrtle. "Listen, we need to stop someplace before we go home."

"Where?"

"Professor Thatcher's home. He was in the library today and invited me to stop by and see his shop. I suggested tomorrow might be better but he was somewhat insistent, so I said okay. Do you know where he lives?"

"I do," said Henri. "It's only a few houses beyond my mother's."

Fifteen minutes later, Henri stopped the car in front of a small, one-story, clapboard house. Next to it was a red wooden barn with what appeared to be an adjoining workshop.

There were lights on in both the house and the workshop.

"He might be in the workshop," said Myrtle, "but let's try the front door first."

Several knocks on the door produced no result.

"Let's check the workshop," said Myrtle. She took Henri's hand and led him around the side of the house.

"He must be in here," she said.

Several more knocks still brought no response.

"I'll peek in the window," said Myrtle.

"Oh, no!" she cried out when she looked inside.

"What is it?" asked Henri, hurrying to her side.

When he looked in he saw Edwin Thatcher slumped in a chair, his head hanging down. He appeared unresponsive.

"Come on," said Henri. He grabbed Myrtle's hand and pulled her back to the door.

Henri tried it and found it unlocked. When they entered they were assaulted by a blast of hot air from the huge fire blazing in the corner fireplace.

"My God, Henri!" exclaimed Myrtle. "It must be a hundred degrees in here!"

"I doubt it's that hot but it sure is warm," said Henri as he hurried to Thatcher's side. "Leave the door open, eh, and open that window, too. Let's cool it off in here."

Henri felt for a pulse—nothing. A gaping hole in Thatcher's chest showed a splatter of blood not yet dried.

"He's dead," said Henri. "His body's still warm."

"I imagine he could have been dead for days and his body would still be warm, as hot as it is in here," said Myrtle, struggling to get the window raised.

"Except he was alive when you saw him earlier today."

"Yes, I didn't mean to imply…oh, never mind."

Henri looked around and spotted a telephone on the wall. "I'll call Doc Sherman and get him over here."

"Tell him to swing by the newspaper office and bring Daisy with him."

"Daisy? What for? And do you even know if she's there?"

"She's there. She told me she'd be working late on a big story. And tell Doctor Sherman to have her bring her Kodak. This is definitely a crime scene; pictures might come in handy."

While Henri was making the call, Myrtle examined the

murder scene. The body was in a captain's chair, feet bound to the chair legs by what appeared to be clothesline, like Mrs. Darling used. Professor Thatcher's hands, lying loose in his lap, also had clothesline loosely wrapped around each of them.

"He must have been able to free his hands sometime while this was all happening," said Henri, rejoining Myrtle.

"Yes, but when?" she asked. "I'm pretty sure he died the instant the knife plunged into his heart. But I don't see any signs of a struggle—no defensive wounds, except for the scratch on his left arm. And I'm not sure he was killed with a knife."

"What do you mean?"

"The wound doesn't look as if a typical knife was used. The opening is more round—not a slit like a normal knife makes."

Henri bent down and looked closer. "I think you're right."

"What kind of weapon might have caused that type of injury?" asked Myrtle.

"The closest I can think of is a railroad spike," said Henri, straightening back up.

"A *railroad* spike?"

"Something like that. You know—the kind of spike they use to secure the rails?"

"Maybe," said Myrtle. "I'm surprised at how he's dressed."

"What do you mean?"

"Long johns and slippers? He knew I was coming. He wouldn't have greeted me dressed like this."

"His pants and shirt and a coat are hanging on the wall over there," said Henri. "And his shoes are on the floor right under them with his socks tucked inside. Maybe he was attacked before he had a chance to get dressed."

"Perhaps," said Myrtle. "You see the stain on his long johns?"

"I didn't want to say anything," said Henri. "I thought he might have had an accident."

"Maybe. Or is it perspiration? It's awfully hot in here still. And look at his hands."

"What are those little white spots all over them?"

"I think the professor had psoriasis," said Myrtle.

"Psoriasis? What's that?"

"A skin disease."

Myrtle indicated a small marble-topped table next to the chair in which Thatcher sat.

"The top is wet. What would have caused that?"

"Maybe he put his hand on it after he got it free and his hand was wet."

"Hmmm," said Myrtle. "Possibly. You know the first name that comes to my mind as to who might have done this, don't you?"

"Who?"

"Declan Murphy."

"You're right," said Henri. "He threatened Professor Thatcher the night of the St. Patrick's Day party."

"And not only that…" Myrtle went on to tell Henri about the incident in town. "But he would've had an accomplice," she concluded.

"What makes you think that?"

"It would take one man to hold the professor down while the other tied him to the chair."

"You're right," said Henri. "So we're looking for two killers."

Just then Doctor Sherman and Daisy arrived.

"Holy wah, it's hot in here!" exclaimed Daisy.

"You should have been here when *we* first arrived," said

Myrtle. "It was like an oven."

"Let's see what we have," said Doctor Sherman, walking over to the professor's body.

"While you're doing that I'm going to see if the house is unlocked," said Henri. "I want to make sure there's no fire in the fireplace. I'll also check to see if I see anything missing."

CHAPTER ELEVEN

A long worktop ran along one wall of the room with a sink and water pump in the middle. While the doctor examined the professor's body, Myrtle and Daisy took note of the items laid out there: a pair of heavy leather gloves; a long-handled tin skillet; a container of partially melted beeswax; eight wicks. Four knives of increasing size lay lined up on a strip of leather. A depression next to the largest knife suggested the set included a fifth. Judging from the size of the other knives Myrtle estimated the missing one to be at least twelve inches in length.

A tapered, tin candle mold with openings for eight fifteen-inch candles lay on its side in the sink in a puddle of water.

Daisy was busy taking pictures of everything.

"Looks like he was getting ready to make some candles," she said.

"Yes. Apparently, he had washed out the candle mold and was preparing to melt the beeswax when he was interrupted," said Myrtle.

"Daisy, I've finished my investigation," said Doctor Sherman. "Why don't you come over here and take some pictures of the body?"

"What do you think, Doc?" asked Henri, who had now returned from the house.

"Cause of death is definitely a single stab wound to the heart. And I mean directly to the heart. He died instantly. Whoever did this knew what they were doing. They knew exactly where the weapon needed to go in; couldn't have been more precise if they'd drawn a bullseye on the man's chest."

"Doctor Sherman," said Myrtle, "I noticed how scaly the professor's arms and hands are, with little spots of white. I think it's psoriasis. What do you think?"

"Yah, psoriasis is my guess. Unusual to find it on hands, but it happens. Henri, can you help me move the body to my sleigh?"

"Okay," said Henri. "I'll make sure the fire is out here before we leave. I'll call Teddy to meet you at your office. He can help you get the body in."

"Your new deputy?" asked Doctor Sherman. "How's he doing?"

"Fine," said Henri. "He's young, twenty-three, but he fought in the war. He knows how to handle himself."

"Why don't you come by my office tomorrow afternoon?" said the doctor. "I'll have the autopsy done by then. Is there anyone who needs to be notified?"

"I'll call Mrs. Darling right after I call Teddy," said Henri. "If anybody knows, she does."

"How did you find the house?" Myrtle asked Henri.

"The fire was almost out. I finished it. I glanced around but didn't see anything out of order. I'll come back tomorrow and take a closer look."

"I'll tell you one thing," said Doctor Sherman, getting ready to go. "I'm pretty sure there was more than one perpetrator."

"That's what Myrtle said," said Henri.

"Really?" said Daisy. "How do you figure that?"

"Think about it," said Myrtle. "How could one person make him sit still while his legs and hands were being bound?"

"Unless he was drugged first;" said Daisy, "or knocked unconscious."

"Well, he wasn't unconscious," said Doctor Sherman. "But drugged? Yah, that's a possibility. I won't know until I do the autopsy. He did get his hands loose before he was stabbed but I didn't find any defensive wounds except that small cut on his arm. I'm betting someone restrained him while he was being tied up."

"Henri said he thinks it looks as if the murder weapon might have been a railroad spike," said Myrtle.

Doctor Sherman cocked his head to one side. "A railroad spike, huh? Perhaps. The wound definitely looks more round, not like a knife did it. I'll know more about that, too, once I've done the autopsy."

"Mrs. Darling says Professor Thatcher has a brother, Orville," said Henri, rejoining the group. "He lives in Greytown but she's not sure where."

Greytown was the neighborhood Myrtle passed through first when she arrived in Booker Falls, a community comprised of identical, modest, two-story, frame structures, each with attic dormer windows and a small porch in front. It was populated for the most part by families of the men who worked in the many mines in the area.

The homes had been built more than fifty years earlier by one of the mines to house its employees.

"So he's a miner?" asked Myrtle.

"No, Mrs. Darling said he used to work on fishing boats

but he's retired now. I'm going to call Eugene. He'll know the address."

"Mr. Littleton, the mail carrier?" asked Daisy.

"Yah," said Henri. "He knows where everybody in town lives."

Moments later, Henri hung up the phone. "I have the address. Myrtle, why don't we drop Daisy off at the newspaper office and you can go on with me to the brother's house. Then I'll take you back to the newspaper office while I go look for Declan."

"Shouldn't you have someone with you?" asked Myrtle.

"I asked Teddy to meet me at my office after he helps Doc Sherman."

*****

As Henri and Myrtle entered Greytown, Myrtle remembered the first time she'd driven through it, what a dull and drab place it appeared to be. All the houses were painted the same gray color, with trim of a darker shade. Most looked as though they hadn't been repainted in the decades since.

Myriad electric lines ran overhead from street poles to each home. To Myrtle, it had looked as though a gigantic fishnet had been tossed over the whole area.

But it had seemed to be a happy neighborhood. It was September, and women were working in their gardens. Children scurried about, dashing in and out of adjoining yards. An old man—the only man she'd seen—sat on his front steps smoking a pipe. He'd waved at her; she waved back.

The second time she'd been in this part of town, she and Henri had gone to interview Paul Momet, who was a suspect in the death of Yvette Sinclair some twenty-eight years earlier. Paul had been found guilty and given a life sentence at the Marquette Branch Prison, the same place Mr. Pfrommer later ended up, when Myrtle, sure Momet had not committed the crime, exposed her housemate Mr. Pfrommer as the true killer.

She was pleased she had been able to prove Momet's innocence but saddened it was at the expense of her friend.

The house where Orville Thatcher lived showed no signs of life. Several knocks at the door brought no response.

"Did Mrs. Darling say if he was married?" asked Myrtle.

"Widowed. She said his wife died in a carriage accident about five years ago."

"Any children?"

"One—a son named Lincoln."

"It seems no one is home," said Myrtle.

Henri pulled out his pocket watch. "It's not quite eight o'clock, yah? Let's see if a neighbor might know where Mr. Thatcher is."

A knock on the door of the adjoining house brought a young woman holding a baby in her arms. A second child, no older than two, clung to her legs.

"Ma'am," said Henri, "I'm Henri de la Cruz, the county constable. I was looking for Mr. Thatcher but he doesn't seem to be home. You wouldn't happen to know where I might find him, would you?"

"No, I have no idea," said the young woman. "I did see him and his son leave earlier today."

"Were they on foot?" asked Myrtle.

"No, dey had a sleigh...which I tought was odd."

"Why did you think it odd?" asked Henri.

"Please," said the woman, "come on in out of da cold."

Once inside, Myrtle looked around. The house was pretty similar to Paul Momet's. A large rug covered the hardwood floor, except for a strip about three feet wide around the outside. Myrtle remembered Henri had told her that under the carpet was cheap pine, but the wood that showed was usually cherry.

A half-dozen photographs hung on one wall. Another wall held two prints——one of Jesus, the other of the Virgin Mary.

Myrtle suspected that it wouldn't be long until more tiny feet were running through the house.

"I tought it odd because Mr. Thatcher, he don't own no sleigh, eh?" She shifted the baby from one arm to the other.

"But you didn't see them come back?" asked Henri.

The woman shook her head. "I did see someone over dere earlier today—after Mr. Thatcher and his son left."

"Do you know who it was?" asked Henri.

"No, he was all bundled up. I don't tink I ever seen him before. He was all wrapped up wit a big scarf 'round his neck; had a chook coverin' his head. I tink he might have been wearin' glasses, but I ain't sure. Couldn't hardly see his face."

"Did the man go into the house?" asked Henri.

"Couldn't say. He walked around da other side, I guess to da back. I din't see him no more after dat."

"I see," said Henri. "Thank you, ma'am. You've been very helpful."

*****

"I should be back in about an hour," said Henri, as Myrtle stepped out of the car in front of the newspaper office.

"What will you do if you find this Murphy fellow?" asked Myrtle.

"Put him in jail for tonight. I'll question him tomorrow."

*****

True to his word, less than an hour later, Henri was back at the newspaper office.

"Did you find him?" asked Myrtle.

"Nah," said Henri. "Teddy and I checked Joker's first. He

said he hadn't seen Murphy in a couple of days, but he'd let me know if he showed up. Then we drove by his house; he wasn't there either. Teddy and I will check again tomorrow."

"What now?"

"Now we go home," said Henri. "I'll come back tomorrow morning and see if I can catch Mr. Thatcher. I want to take a closer look at Edwin Thatcher's place, too. And Doc Sherman should have the autopsy done by the afternoon."

"Can I come with you? I don't have to work."

"Why do you want to come?" asked Henri.

"Why? For one thing, four eyes are better than two if you're snooping around in the deceased Mr. Thatcher's home. And don't forget who helped you solve five other murders over the last three years."

Henri sighed. How could he forget? Whenever she needed something, she reminded him of it. At first, he resented her inserting herself into the investigations. Now, he realized, he looked forward to having her around.

"All right," he said. "But remember—I'm the one who's in charge."

"Of course, you are," said Myrtle, looking away so Henri couldn't see the grin on her face.

CHAPTER TWELVE

After a quick breakfast of corned beef hash, two poached eggs, toast, and coffee, Myrtle disappeared upstairs to brush her teeth, comb her hair and perform all the duties a woman has to do before she can be seen out in public.

When she came back downstairs, Henri was waiting at the door.

"Finally ready?" he asked.

Myrtle gave him her sweetest smile. "Yes, sir, I am."

"Daisy's in the car. We'll drop her off at the newspaper office. She said she's going to develop the pictures she took last night; she can have them done by this afternoon."

"Ain't modern technology wonderful?" said Myrtle.

*****

Once again, there was no response at Orville's house when Henri knocked.

A quick trip next door to the same young woman elicited the information that, as far as she was aware, Orville and his son had not returned to the house since they'd left the previous day.

"What now?" asked Myrtle.

"Now we go back to Edwin Thatcher's house. I hoped to secure Orville's permission to search the place, but I don't need it since it's a crime scene."

*****

They found the workshop much as it had been the night before except for the temperature.

"Good Lord, Henri, it's *freezing* in here!" exclaimed Myrtle. "Can we have a fire?"

"Go ahead," said Henri.

Myrtle looked at him. "Me? Why me? You're the man."

Henri had to suppress a smile. "And you're the independent woman. I'm fine. If you want a fire, make one."

"Hmmph," grunted Myrtle. "Forget it."

"Then let's collect the evidence," said Henri. "Maybe that will warm you up. Afterward, we'll check out the barn."

"What are we taking?" asked Myrtle.

Henri looked around. "Just the clothesline, I guess. I don't see anything else that's relevant."

"The knives," said Myrtle, gathering up the four knives and placing them into a sack. "Let's take these. The missing one could be the murder weapon."

"Okay, let's take them," said Henri. "But the way Doc Sherman explained the wound, it doesn't sound like it. Leave everything else just as it is."

Numerous bales of hay, a scruffy sleigh, and an even shabbier carriage were the primary occupants of the main floor of the barn. In one corner was a stall where a bay-colored Morgan poked its head over the door.

"Oh, my, Henri, that poor horse. Won't it freeze to death? It's as cold in here as it was in the workshop."

"No, horses are fine in cold weather as long as they're protected from any wind. But it will require someone to feed it. I'll have Andy take care of it." He looked up at the loft. "Let's see what's up there, eh?"

Myrtle followed Henri up the wooden ladder that led to a floor covering more than half the barn. As they approached the top, Myrtle stopped.

"You hear that sound?" she asked.

Henri also stopped. "Yah–some kind of buzzing."

When they reached the top, they stopped and gazed in wonder at a half-dozen beehives in the middle of the floor, surrounded by bales of hay.

"Oh, oh," said Myrtle. "That's where the buzzing's coming from."

"I guess if he has beeswax he must have bees," said Henri.

"Should we leave?" asked Myrtle.

"Nah. I think they must be hibernating or something. It's winter—where they going to go?"

Henri walked over to the edge of the floor where a block and tackle had been installed. Several buckets sat scattered about.

"He must use this to move the hives in the spring," he said. "And take the beeswax down, too, I warrant; safer than trying it on the ladder."

"I've seen enough," said Myrtle, feeling none too comfortable in the company of so many possible enemies. "Let's check out the house. I want to see if the missing knife is there."

As with the workshop and barn, the house was unheated. Remnants of the fire Henri had extinguished the night before lay in the fireplace.

"Why don't you take the bathroom first?" said Henri. "I'll check the kitchen."

"Okay. Don't forget your gloves."

*****

"Did you find anything?" Myrtle asked when she and Henri met a few minutes later in the parlor.

"I found knives but none that matched the ones from the workshop. You?"

"I found this."

Myrtle handed Henri a bottle half-full of liquid.

"What is it?" he asked.

"The label says it's morphine—prescribed by a Dr. Järvinen in Hancock."

"He must have been pretty sick to be taking morphine," said Henri.

"Yes, perhaps Doctor Sherman can tell us after he's done the autopsy. Why don't I check out the study, eh, while you take a look in the bedroom and the parlor?"

Myrtle felt like an intruder going through the files and letters piled up on Edwin Thatcher's roll-top desk and stuffed into the many drawers and cubby holes. Finding nothing of interest, she was about to give up when she noticed a folder in the bottom of the last drawer.

She picked it up and read the words across the top: *Last Will and Testament.*

"Henri, I found something!" she yelled out.

"What?" Henri yelled back from the parlor.

"I'll bring it out. I want to take a look at the bookshelves first."

Myrtle walked over to the shelves that took up one wall and scanned the titles: reference books, manuals, encyclopedias, dictionaries, books of maps, history books—no fiction.

"Did you find anything?" she asked when she joined Henri in the parlor.

"Nothing that would help the investigation," said Henri. "What did you find?"

Myrtle handed Henri the folder.

"This."

"A will? Did you look at it?" asked Henri.

"No, I thought you should."

Henri removed a single sheet of paper from the folder and read it silently.

"What does it say?" asked Myrtle.

"It says Thatcher left everything he owned, all his possessions, to his nephew, Lincoln."

Myrtle's eyebrows lifted. "Mmm. I guess that might make him a suspect, eh? That would be a motive. When is it dated?"

Henri glanced at the paper. "A month ago."

"Only a month. It would be interesting to know what moved him to write it."

"Or change it," said Henri. "Maybe this is not his first will ever."

"Maybe," said Myrtle. "Oh, look . . ."

She walked over to a table next to an easy chair and picked up a book that was lying there.

"This is the book Professor Thatcher checked out yesterday morning."

"What is it?" asked Henri.

"An anatomy book."

"An anatomy book? Wonder why he wanted that."

"I don't know. But I might as well take it with me back to the library."

"Yah, he sure won't be needing it anymore," said Henri.

"Where to now?" asked Myrtle.

"We'll stop by my office; see if Teddy has any news on Declan. Oh, and the professor named you the executor of his will."

"What?" cried Myrtle as Henri walked out of the room.

CHAPTER THIRTEEN

Thanks to Myrtle, Henri's office had been updated considerably since she arrived in Booker Falls. The formerly white walls were now peach. There were four chairs instead of just the one that had been there before—although it did make it a bit more crowded. A photograph of President Warren G. Harding had replaced that of his predecessor, Woodrow Wilson. Curtains had been installed over the one window. The filing cabinet had been moved to the storage room at the end of the hall, just beyond the two jail cells.

One addition Henri had made himself: a copper lamp with a curved base and a fringe of colored tubes dangling from the bronze shade. It was a replacement for a brass postmaster desk lamp that had definitely seen better days.

But some things were the same: the small desk on which the lamp sat, a desk chair on its last legs, and the wall telephone that was jangling when Henri entered the room.

"Hello," he said, grabbing the mouthpiece off its cradle.

"Henri, it's Teddy," came the voice from the other end. "I'm at the train depot. Declan Murphy and another fellow are hanging around outside."

"Keep your eye on them and don't let them leave," said Henri. "I'm on my way." He replaced the phone in the cradle and turned to Myrtle. "You stay here. I'll be back shortly."

*****

"Where are they?"

Henri had driven as fast as he could to get to the train depot before Declan had any chance of leaving. And who was the man with Declan? Doc Sherman said he thought there were two killers. Maybe this other man was Murphy's accomplice.

"Over there by that freight car," said Teddy, nodding in that direction.

"Come on," said Henri.

"Declan Murphy?" said Henri when they reached the two men.

"Who wants to know?" Murphy growled, turning to see who had called out to him.

"Constable de la Cruz," replied Henri.

"Eh, Constable," said Murphy. His tone softened. He remembered his two previous encounters with Henri. "What can I do for you?"

"Where were you last night around five o'clock?"

"Why?"

"Just answer the question," said Henri.

"If you must know, I spent da whole night at Noé's."

"And who is Noé?" asked Teddy.

"Dat's me," said the man standing next to Murphy. His tone of voice wasn't as pleasant.

"What were you two doing?" asked Henri.

"Gettin' drunk as a skunk," said Murphy, laughing. "Hell, we's still drunk. We come out here to see if'n old man Weston had any coffee."

"Yah, but he didn't," said Noé. "So's we was debatin' what

to do. Maybe go over to da Hungry Hog."

"I'll get you coffee," said Henri.

"You will?" said Murphy.

"Yah, down at the jail. I'm taking you both in."

"You're arrestin' us?" asked Noé. "What for? We ain't *dat* drunk."

"That's for the judge to decide," said Henri. "You two got any weapons on you?"

Murphy glanced down at the empty knife sheath on his belt. "Guess not," he said.

"How about you, Noé?" asked Teddy.

Noé shook his head. "Not unless you count my fists. I tink I could kill you both wit my bare hands if I had a hankerin' to."

Henri's and Teddy's hands went to their guns.

"We'll make sure you don't get a hankering to," said Henri. "Come on let's go."

After handcuffing both men, Teddy marched them down the street toward the jail, while Henri drove alongside. Passersby stopped and stared as the parade passed, the women shaking their heads in disapproval.

*****

"Tell me again why I should give you warrants to search those two men's homes?"

Henri had called Judge Hurstbourne at home asking for warrants to search both Murphy's and Noé's houses.

"I'm looking for the murder weapon that was used to kill Edwin Thatcher," said Henri. "We suspect it may have been a railroad spike. Teddy and I found Murphy and his buddy hanging around the train depot this morning. Their alibi for when the professor was killed is that they were together at Noés. I also want to see if I find any clothesline that matches what was used to tie up the professor, and anything they may have stolen from his house or workshop."

"But why do you suspect them in the first place?"

Henri explained about the two incidents when Murphy threatened Thatcher.

"He was the one who caused the ruckus at the Chili Cook-Off, too," added Henri. "He's a troublemaker. And Doc Sherman says he thinks there were two perpetrators. I believe Noé could be the second man."

"Well, okay then," said the judge, "that's good enough for me. I'll be down at my office in an hour. You can get your warrants then. What's this Noé's last name?"

"Virtanen," said Henri. He hung up the phone.

"Teddy, you stay here and keep an eye on things. Myrtle and I are going to take another run at Orville Thatcher's place."

*****

This time they found Orville at home.

Other than being the same height and approximate weight, there was little to tell that Edwin and Orville Thatcher were brothers.

While Edwin's facial hair consisted only of his handlebar mustache and long sideburns, Orville's beard extended a good eight inches below his chin. And while Edwin's salt-and-pepper hair was cut short, Orville sported a six-inch pigtail, a memento of his days spent on fishing boats.

Myrtle thought Orville took the news of his brother's death better than she would have expected. He didn't even ask how he had been killed or if there were any suspects.

"Were the two of you close?" she asked.

Orville shook his head. "Not really. It's a long story."

"Was it over your wife?" asked Myrtle.

Orville looked at her in surprise. "You know 'bout dat?" His shoulders slumped. "I s'pose everyone in town knows about it. Edwin tought I stole Caroline out from under him when he was away at school. Troot is, we'd already fallen in love. Den when da accident happened...well, dat seemed to be da straw dat broke da camel's back, if ya know what I mean. We ain't been much on speakin' terms since den. And it din't get no better when da whole ting 'bout da cabin come up."

"What was that?" asked Henri.

"My Pa, he was a miner. But him and Mama wanted someting better for me and Edwin. So Edwin, he went off to college and got his degree. I wasn't da college type. I liked fishin', ya know? So I worked on da fishin' boats over out of Portage Lake. Dat was my life. Pa owned a cabin dere and dat's where I stayed durin' da fishin' season.

"When Pa died fifteen years ago he left dis house to me and da cabin on Portage Lake to Edwin, with da understandin' dat Mama could continue to live here wit me and Caroline until she died and I could use da cabin during da fishin' season so's I wouldn't have to make dat long trek back here. Edwin already had his cottage over dere at da college, ya know.

"Den, when Mama passed seven years ago, Edwin kicked me out o' da cabin; said I couldn't use it no more. Dat meant no more fishin' for me, 'cause I din't have no other place to stay. I had to quit; I wasn't near ready to quit."

"That must have made you angry," said Henri.

"Yah, I was pretty mad. But what're ya gonna do?"

Myrtle had been looking around the room while Orville was talking. The walls were blank: no pictures and no mirrors. The single photograph visible was one on the mantle of two men standing side by side. She walked over and picked it up.

"Is this you and your son?" she asked.

"Oh, yah," said Orville. "We had dat took a month after Caroline's funeral. She and I never had no picture took—couldn't afford it. But after she died I tought Lincoln and I should have one together. Dat way, when I'm gone, at least he can remember what I looked like."

"And where does Lincoln live?" asked Henri.

"Oh, he lives here wit me, now. He used to have his own fishin' boat, but tree years ago it sunk in a storm. He din't have no insurance, so he couldn't replace it. Fact is, he still owes Joker for da money he loaned him to buy da boat."

The front door opened and Lincoln entered. One of his eyes was blackened. Orville introduced Henri and Myrtle and told Lincoln why they were there.

"Do you know of anyone who would want to hurt your brother?" Henri asked Orville once they were all seated again.

Orville shook his head. "Not dat I can tink of. Like I said, I ain't had much contact wit Edwin in years so I don't know none of his friends or who he hangs out wit. Lincoln's been kinda friendly wit him."

"You were close to your uncle?" Myrtle asked Lincoln.

"Yah, I didn't let da blow-up 'tween him and my dad affect our relationship. I'd stop by every couple weeks to see him. We'd talk about da bees and how he got da honey and made candles. He'd show me how to write better. Most of da time we talked about Mama, even after she was gone."

"Did you know he left everything to you in his will?" asked Henri.

"Yah, he told me a few weeks back."

"Better Lincoln dan dat woman," said Orville.

"Woman?" said Myrtle.

"My uncle was seeing a woman—engaged, actually," said Lincoln. "But he broke it off."

"Do you know why?" asked Henri.

Lincoln shook his head. "No idea. I knowed she wasn't real happy 'bout it. I was dere when it happened. I was in da kitchen and dey was in da parlor. Uncle Edwin told her dey was troo and he had changed his will and she was out of it. She got to yellin' and screamin' someting fierce, said he'd be sorry, she'd make sure of dat. After she left dat's when he told me about da new will, dat I was gettin' everyting."

"Everyting 'cept da cabin," said Orville. "Lincoln said Edwin said he was goin' to sell it."

"Do you know the woman's name?" Henri asked Lincoln.

"Just her first name—Tallulah. She lived a couple blocks down da street from Uncle Edwin."

"There can't be many Tallulah's in Booker Falls," said Myrtle.

"How'd you get the black eye?" asked Henri.

"Joker," said Lincoln. "I owe him some money. Dis was his gentle reminder dat he wanted it and he wanted it now. I told him, just be patient—I'd be getting' some money real soon."

"Mr. Thatcher, I came back last night and again this morning and you weren't here. Where were you?" asked Henri.

"Lincoln and me, we went over to da cabin. Edwin had asked me to meet him dere. I figgered since he was sellin' da place, maybe he wanted me to move my stuff out."

"When did he ask you to meet him?" asked Myrtle.

"Yesterday. Young feller stopped by wit a note. Said it was important dat we meet dere last night. But Edwin, he never showed up. Guess I know why, now. Lincoln and me stayed da night; got back dis mornin'."

"Lincoln went with you?" asked Myrtle.

"Yah. I don't have no sleigh or car, so Lincoln borrowed Mr. Middleton's sleigh."

"Malcolm Middleton?" said Henri. "Isn't he out of town right now?"

"Yah," said Orville. "In Floreeda. Lincoln's lookin' after da place, don't ya know, takin' care o' da horses and such."

"Do you still have the note?" asked Myrtle.

"Nah. Troo it in da fireplace at da cabin when I saw Edwin wasn't comin'. I was pretty upset dat we made dat long trip for nothin'."

"And the two of you spent the night there?" asked Henri.

"Yah. It was too late to come back."

"Mr. Thatcher, when was the last time you saw your brother?" asked Henri.

"Five years ago, at Caroline's funeral. But we din't talk. He din't even say hello to me or sorry for your loss or nothin'."

"The professor had several run-ins with a man by the name of Declan Murphy over the last few months," said Myrtle. "Do you know him?"

"Oh, yah, dat man, he always was trouble, even as a kid. Declan's family, dey lived in da house right behind us. Lincoln and him is about da same age."

"You were friends?" Henri asked Lincoln.

"I wouldn't 'zactly say friends. Pa wouldn't let him come in our yard."

"Yah," said Orville. "I run him off lots of times. I knowed he was sneakin' into my shed and stealin' stuff. Da last time I near beat da little bugger to death wit a big wooden spoon. He never come back after dat."

"When was the last time either of you saw him?" asked Henri.

"I ain't seed him in years," said Orville. "Not since his ma and pa both passed away."

"Dat was when deir house burned down," added Lincoln.

"Yah. Richie Barnoble tought maybe Declan did it. I did too. But dey couldn't prove nothin'."

"I saw Declan a couple months ago," said Lincoln. "I was havin' a beer at Joker's when he come in and sat down next to me. He was already drunk. He started going on and on about how he hated Pa, saying some day he was going to get even wit him for dat beating."

"You never said nothin' 'bout dat to me," said Orville.

"I didn't want to upset you. 'Sides, it was just a crazy drunk rattlin' on."

"Again, I am sorry for your loss," said Henri. "Doc Sherman will get in touch with you about what to do with the body."

*****

"What do you think about Declan?" asked Myrtle when she and Henri were back in the car.

"I think we need to take a serious look at him," said Henri.

"Yes, me, too. But you know what doesn't make sense?"

"What's that?"

"Why would Professor Thatcher ask his brother to meet him at the cabin when he had already asked me to come to his home? He couldn't have been in both places."

"Good question," said Henri.

CHAPTER FOURTEEN

"Good timing," said Doctor Sherman as he ushered Henri and Myrtle into his office. "I've just finished the autopsy."

"What did you find?" asked Myrtle.

"He definitely died from whatever he was stabbed with. I'm not sure what the murder weapon was but as I said last night, it's unlikely it was an ordinary knife. Like Henri said, something more like a spike. There was no bruising anywhere so even though he'd freed his hands I didn't find any evidence of a struggle other than that small cut on his arm. It was fresh so it *could* have happened during a scuffle. Now, here's a couple things of interest, eh? Around the entry wound there was a little bit of soot mixed in with the blood."

"Soot?" said Henri.

"Yah, from the fireplace, I reckon. The killer might have marked the spot so he'd know exactly where to insert the weapon."

"You said there were a couple of things?" said Myrtle.

"Professor Thatcher was dying of cancer."

"He had *cancer*?" said Henri.

"Yah. And from the looks of it, I'd say he had no more

than a few months to live, either."

"That explains the morphine," said Myrtle.

"So," said Henri, "whoever killed him—if they'd only waited a bit he would have died a natural death."

"That's about it," said the doctor.

"Did you find any drugs in his system?" asked Myrtle.

"Nah," said Doc Sherman. "Nothing but the morphine."

*****

After a quick bite at Miss Madeline's, Henri and Myrtle got Tallulah's last name and address from Mrs. Littlefield at the post office. Then they stopped at the judge's office, picked up the two warrants, and drove to Declan's home.

After an hour of searching, the only item they found that might prove relevant to the case was the knife missing from Declan's sheath when he was picked up.

A stop at Noé's home proved more fruitful.

"Look at this," said Myrtle.

A ten-foot-long canvas lean-to was attached to an outside wall of the house, the top part held up by nails, the bottom part secured by four stakes pounded into the ground. A jumble of various items lay stacked up underneath.

"What are you looking at?" asked Henri.

"Those stakes—I don't know how deep they go down but I bet they're long enough to stab someone with."

Henri bent over and, with some effort, pulled up a stake. It appeared to be at least a foot long.

"You're right," he said. "Let's see if we can find any others."

A quick check of the shed behind the house turned up seven additional stakes. Further searching in the shed and the house produced nothing more.

"I'm not surprised we didn't find any clothesline," said Myrtle as they returned to the car.

"Why not?" asked Henri.

"First of all, neither one of the houses had clothesline strung up in the back yard. And, secondly, from the way those two looked and smelled, I doubt if they ever bothered to wash their clothes."

*****

Located on the other side of town near the college and three blocks from Edwin's home, Tallulah Redman's cottage had seen better days. Everything about it appeared in need of repair. Even the wooden fence out front was missing more boards than were present.

The woman who answered the door was marginally attractive, in her sixties with flaming red hair and wearing an overabundance of makeup. Myrtle didn't think she seemed to be Edwin Thatcher's type at all.

Once inside the house, Myrtle understood why Tallulah was wearing a heavy coat with a knitted chook and a matching scarf wrapped around her neck. The temperature in the room couldn't have been more than fifty-five. Myrtle was happy she had on her skunk skin coat.

"That's a beautiful scarf you have on," said Myrtle.

"Oh, tank you, dearie. I made it meself."

"You knit?"

"Yah," said Tallulah. "I sure do."

"What else do you make?" asked Myrtle.

"Oh, everting. Dat's how I make my livin', ya know, what little of it dere is—scarves, trows, blankets, sweaters, gloves, shawls, caps—even rugs. I make dem all."

"I think I've seen some of your work at the women's wear store downtown," said Myrtle.

"Yah, Mrs. Dougherty, she buys dem from me. Her and udder stores around. Like I said, ain't much, but it helps. So, what's dis about, Constable? Why you here?"

"It's about Professor Thatcher," said Henri. "He was found dead last night in his workshop."

For a minute Tallulah just sat and stared at Henri as though she didn't understand what he'd said. Then she burst into tears, sobbing, rocking back and forth.

She's more taken by his death than his brother was, thought Henri.

"How did it happen?" asked Tallulah when she finally regained her composure.

Henri explained what they thought had occurred.

"Murder?" asked Tallulah, a shocked look on her face. "Do ya know who done it?"

"Not yet," said Henri.

"Do you know of anyone who would want to harm the professor?" asked Myrtle.

"Yah, dat brudder of his. Dey din't git along, you know."

"So I gathered," said Henri.

"Did you know the professor had cancer?" asked Henri.

"Cancer? I never knowed he had cancer," said Tallulah. "He never said nothin' to me 'bout no cancer. You sure?"

"Doctor Sherman confirmed it," said Henri.

"Who's takin' care of Elmore? And da bees?" asked Tallulah.

"Who's Elmore?" asked Myrtle.

"Edwin's horse."

"Oh," said Henri, "I have Andy Erickson looking in on him for now. I reckon it will be Lincoln's responsibility once the will is read."

A scowl crossed Tallulah's face. "All dat shoulda been mine," she said. "Edwin said he was gonna leave me everting. We was gonna git married. Den he ups and breaks up wit me and tells me Lincoln's gettin' everting. It ain't fair."

She softened almost as quickly as her anger had flared up.

"I'll look in on da bees," she said. "Dey ain't gonna be very active 'til it gets warmer, but I'll stop by dere and take a look-see."

"Miss Redman, where were you last night around five o'clock?" asked Myrtle.

"It's Mrs. Redman—I'm widowed; seven years now. Why you wanna know where I was?"

"Just routine," said Myrtle.

"I was right here—playin' fifteen-two all evenin' wit Carl."

"Carl?" said Henri.

"My brudder," said Tallulah.

"Does Carl live here with you?" asked Henri.

"He does now. Moved in 'bout four months ago, right after he got out o' da prison over dere in Marquette."

"He was in prison?" asked Myrtle. "What for?"

"Manslaughter; served eight years. Killed a feller in a bar fight. But he's good now."

"Is he here now?" asked Henri.

"Nah. He's probably down at Joker's gettin' shit-faced."

*****

"What do you think?" asked Myrtle when she and Henri were back in the car.

"She certainly had motive."

"Two motives——first, that the professor broke off their engagement, and second that he wrote her out of his will. You need to ask Judge Hurstbourne for a search warrant."

"Why? You think we might find the missing knife there?"

Myrtle shook her head. "I think you can forget about the knife for now. It doesn't look as though it was the murder weapon."

"Then what do you think we might find?"

"Maybe clothesline—for sure a needle."

Henri looked at her. "A needle?"

"You heard what she said about her knitting?"

"Yah. So what?"

"Do you know what you use to do knitting?" asked Myrtle.

Henri shrugged. "I have no idea."

"Needles—knitting needles."

"I don't think you could kill someone with a little needle," said Henri.

"Those aren't little needles. Some are a foot long or more—and pretty big in circumference."

"You think she might have killed the professor with a knitting needle?"

"It's a possibility."

"I didn't know you knew how to knit," said Henri.

"I don't," said Myrtle, "but Mrs. Darling does. She showed me her different knitting needles once. One of the larger ones might well be our murder weapon."

"But you saw how she cried when we told her about the professor."

"Henri, do you remember the play we saw at the theatre last month?"

"Sure. It was fun," said Henri.

"Do you remember the actress who played the role of Agnes's aunt, Aunt Mary? You said you thought it was some of the best acting you'd ever seen."

"Aunt Mary? Yah, I thought she did a terrific job. She sure could act up a storm."

"That was Tallulah."

*****

That evening, back at the boarding house, Myrtle, Henri, and Daisy all retired to the parlor after dinner.

"Let's take a look at Daisy's pictures," said Henri.

He and Myrtle had been so busy driving from one place to

another they had completely forgotten to stop at the newspaper office to pick up the photographs Daisy had taken at the crime scene, so she had brought them home with her.

For the next fifteen minutes they passed them around from one to the other.

Myrtle was the first to comment.

"There's something wrong here," she said, "but I can't put my finger on it."

"I don't see anything out of the ordinary," said Daisy.

"Me neither," said Henri.

"Well, there's something," said Myrtle, laying the last photograph down on the table. "Hopefully it will come to me."

CHAPTER FIFTEEN

The next morning after securing a warrant from Judge Hurstbourne, Henri picked up Teddy and the two of them drove to Tallulah's home.

"You wanta search my home?" she asked when Henri explained why they were there. "What for?"

"Several items," said Henri, "including your knitting needles."

"My *knittin'* needles?" asked Tallulah. "What in da world for?"

"Please go get them," said Henri. "Teddy, you check the shed out back. I'll wait here."

Tallulah brought out a cloth bag filled with various items including several long, wooden knitting needles.

Henri removed the six largest needles and slipped them into a bag he'd brought with him.

"I'm going to have to take these," he said.

"Whaddya mean, take 'em?" asked Tallulah, visibly upset. "I need dose to do my knittin'."

"You'll get them back once we're through with them," said Henri.

"Troo wit dem? What, you gonna take up knittin'?"

"No, they could be evidence in Professor Thatcher's murder."

"Evidence? What—you tink I bumped off dat ol' S.O.B.?"

"Did you?" asked Henri.

"Heck, no!" shouted Tallulah. "I loved dat ol' man, even if he did do me wrong."

"You were angry with him for breaking up with you and for cutting you out of his will. And you don't have an alibi."

"I weren't angry enough to kill him. And I do too have a alibi. I told you me and Carl was here playin' fifteen-two."

"Right now I'm not sure that's a good enough alibi," said Henri.

By this time Teddy had returned from the shed.

"Find anything?" asked Henri.

Teddy shook his head. "No clothesline, nothing else that seemed suspicious."

*****

"What now?" asked Teddy after he and Henri had escaped the house and Tallulah's wrath.

"Let's go back to the office," said Henri. "I want to interrogate Declan and Noé separately."

After dropping off the knitting needles at the doctor's office, Henri spent the next hour questioning Declan who stuck to his story that he had spent the entire evening at Noé's home getting drunk. He barely remembered who the professor was, he said. The two incidents that Henri brought up were so insignificant that he said he wouldn't recognize Thatcher if he met him on the street.

Noé said the same thing.

"What can you tell me about this?" asked Henri, laying a stake from Noé's place on the desk.

"Where'd you get dat?" asked Noé.

"It came from your home. There were ten more just like it. Where did you get them?"

"My daddy," said Noé. "He give 'em to me."

"Your daddy, huh?" said Henri. "And where did he get them?"

"He was in da war—da Civil War; a quartermaster. Dose were stakes from da quartermaster's tent."

"How many stakes were there?"

"Twelve—six on each side o' da tent."

"I found eleven at your home," said Henri. "What happened to the other one?"

Noé shrugged. "I dunno. I don't keep track o' dem."

"Tell me why you did it," said Henri. "Why'd you kill the professor?"

"Kill da perfessor? What perfessor? I don't know what you're talkin' 'bout."

"Professor Edwin Thatcher. I think you and Declan killed him, and you used one of these stakes to do it."

"Dat's crazy!" cried Noé. "We din't kill no perfessor. When was he kilt?"

"Last night."

"Last night? We already told you we was gettin' drunk at my place."

"Yah, that's what Declan said, too, but I don't believe you."

"It's da truth whether you believe me or not."

"What do you think?" asked Teddy after Noé was placed back in his cell.

"They seem pretty set on their stories," said Henri. "I'm not sure. They're going before Judge Hurstbourne this morning. He'll give them a couple of weeks for public drunkenness. That will give us some time to dig a little deeper. I'm going to go over to Doc Sherman's office and leave these stakes for him to look at and also see what he can tell me about Mrs. Redman's knitting needles. Tomorrow I'll go back and get the rest of the stakes, see if I can find the one that's unaccounted for."

*****

"Couldn't find a trace of blood on any of them," said Doctor Sherman, when Henri asked about the knitting needles. "One of them could be the murder weapon or one similar to them. Can't tell for sure. I'll take a look at these stakes and let you know."

*****

Henri was waiting in the kitchen for Myrtle when George dropped her off after picking her up at the library.

While Myrtle ate the fried chicken and mashed potatoes Mrs. Darling had left warming for her on the stove, he filled her in on his visit with Tallulah, and how upset she was he had taken her knitting needles.

"I can understand that;" said Myrtle between bites, "but you had to. Has Doctor Sherman had a chance to look at them yet?"

"Yah, he didn't find any blood on any of them. But I'm not sure she gave me all the big ones, either. I questioned Declan and Noé some more but I didn't get anything more out of them."

"What about those stakes we found?" asked Myrtle. "What did Noé have to say about those?"

Henri repeated what Noé had told him about the stakes having belonged to his father.

"I'm sending Teddy out there tomorrow to see if he can find the one that's missing."

"I think you should tell him to get the ones up out of the ground, too. If one of those was used to kill the professor they might have been smart enough to put it back into the ground."

Henri nodded. "I will. Now, you ready for another chalkboard meeting?"

Myrtle looked at him, confused.

"What are you talking about?" she asked.

"You remember when you and George and I met with Jake at his office and used his chalkboard to try to figure out who killed the Steinmyers and Rudy Folger?"

"Ah, yes, I remember," said Myrtle. She picked up her glass, took a drink of milk, then set the glass back down. "I also recall that the process never helped us figure out the real killer's identity."

Henri grinned. "Yah, I believe you're right there. Nevertheless, when I talked with Jake today and showed him everything we had, he thought we should give it another go. We're going to meet tomorrow evening, and he'd like you there if you're game."

"Same people as last time?"

"Not George; he's going to be out of town. But Teddy will join us."

"Sure," said Myrtle as she popped one last bite of chicken into her mouth. "I'm game."

CHAPTER SIXTEEN

Henri studied the photographs spread out before him on his desk. What was it Myrtle saw that concerned her?

It seemed pretty clear to him. Edwin Thatcher was in his workshop. He was preparing to melt some beeswax to pour into the candle molds. The room was unusually hot because of the roaring blaze in the fireplace. Was that why he was dressed only in his long johns and slippers? He had asked Myrtle to come by after she got off work, so he surely would have been more properly attired before her arrival.

Someone had surprised him—someone he knew? Declan? Tallulah? Doc Sherman said he thought there must have been two perpetrators. If it were Declan, then Noé would more than likely have been the other man. They would have overpowered Edwin, tied him to the chair, then stabbed him with something that might have been shaped like a railroad spike. There'd been no evidence of a scuffle, Doc said, although Edwin did have that one cut on his arm.

Somehow he had gotten both hands free before he was stabbed and killed. But what had occurred between the time he was tied up and then? Were the two intruders looking for something? There was no sign they had tortured the professor. If it *were* Declan and Noé, they could have passed the time drinking beer. But where would they have gotten it? Henri had seen no sign of it either in the workshop or the house. Might they have brought it with them?

There was no question Declan had the motive. He'd had two run-ins with the professor, both of which ended in him being humiliated. He and Teddy had found nothing when they searched his home. But there *were* the stakes at Noé's place.

He didn't believe Mrs. Redman was much of a suspect even though she was upset about the professor breaking off their engagement. And even more upset, Henri thought, that he'd written her out of his will. She couldn't have killed the professor by herself; but there was the matter of her brother. Some checking on Henri's part had revealed that his recent stint for manslaughter had not been his first run-in with the law.

How about the knitting needles? Doctor Sherman said one of them *could* have been the murder weapon.

And then there was the question of Orville and Lincoln Thatcher.

They both had motives: Orville was angry at his brother about being kicked out of the cabin while Lincoln stood to inherit everything Edwin owned. He certainly needed the money with Joker pressing him to pay back a loan. It was well known Joker could be very persuasive when it came time to collect what people owed him.

Lincoln and his father could have easily subdued Edwin, tied him up, and killed him. Their alibi was that they'd been at the cabin all night. But when did they leave town? Did anyone see them at the cabin? Until they were questioned further, it wasn't much of an alibi.

As far as alibis went, Declan and Noé claimed they were together drinking beer. But who could corroborate that? And Mrs. Redman said she and her brother spent the evening playing cribbage. Could anyone confirm that?

Right now, thought Henri, *I still have six suspects, all with motives, none of whom have solid alibis.*

He yawned, stretched, got up from behind his desk, walked over to the window, pulled back the curtains, and gazed out at the nearly deserted street.

Snow still covered everything but it was clear spring was on its way. The small rose of Sharon shrub outside the window had begun to bud. Beads of water dripped from icicles that had formed on the eaves of the building across the street.

From his literature class at Adelaide over ten years ago Henri remembered the words of Tennyson: "In the spring a young man's fancy lightly turns to thoughts of love."

Well, he wasn't a young man for sure. But he definitely was having thoughts of love. Last month he had asked Myrtle to be his wife. She hadn't said yes, but she hadn't said no, either.

How strange, he thought, *that I've come to this point of being so deeply in love with her.*

When she'd first arrived in town—and almost ran him over with her car—his thoughts of her had been nothing but negative. And when she repeatedly inserted herself into his murder investigations he was, at first, irritated, then just plain angry. He had always found her attractive. But it was a gradual, subtle process in which he discovered just how much she meant to him, how fond of her he'd become.

Had he waited too long to let her know how much he loved her—enough to want to marry her?

He had heard rumors that George had also proposed to her.

What had been her answer to him? Since he'd not heard of any plans for their wedding, he could only assume she had either given him the same answer he'd received or, better yet, she had refused his offer.

The voice coming from one of the jail cells brought him out of his reverie.

"Hey, Constable, when do we get our breakfast?"

Henri turned and walked down the hall to the first cell.

"Why? You hungry?" he asked Murphy, who was standing at the bars to his cell.

"Hell yes, we're hungry," said Murphy. "We're entitled to three meals a day while you got us locked up in here. If you had any compassion you'd give us some beer, too."

Henri chuckled. "I'll call over to Miss Madeline's and get some food sent over."

"What about the beer?" asked Noé from the adjoining cell.

"You're lucky you're getting coffee," said Henri, walking back to his office. "It could just be water."

CHAPTER SEVENTEEN

In his late thirties and a graduate of the University of Michigan Law School, Jake McIntyre had served for the past decade as the prosecuting attorney for this part of Michigan's Upper Peninsula.

At five-foot-seven and well over two hundred pounds, he didn't cut an imposing figure. But his prowess as a prosecutor was well known. Short, fat, and bald was how his enemies—and more than a few of his friends—described him. But everyone agreed he was a lion in the courtroom.

Jake licked his lips at the prospect of trying another murder. This would be his fourth murder case in less than three years. Life was looking up!

Using a wet rag, he meticulously wiped clean the chalkboard that took up a large portion of one wall of his office. When he finished, he hung the rag on a hook in the bathroom, then walked to the sideboard set against another wall and checked the four glasses sitting there to ensure they were spotless.

He picked up the bottle of scotch to make sure it was full. He looked forward to this meeting today.

A knock on the door caused him to turn and look; it was Henri and Myrtle.

"Come on in," said Jake. "Teddy should be here any minute."

Almost as if on cue, Teddy appeared behind Henri and Myrtle.

"Good, good;" said Jake, "we're all here. Scotch, anyone?"

"Pour me one," said Henri.

"Me, too," said Myrtle. "Mrs. Darling was kind enough to send a pasty with Henri so I don't have to drink on an empty stomach."

"How about you, Teddy?" asked Jake as he poured three drinks.

Teddy hesitated for a minute and didn't answer.

"You're not a teetotaler, are you?" asked Jake.

"No, sir, I'm not. It's just that…well, it *is* Prohibition, eh?"

"Son," said Jake, "Prohibition prohibits the production, importation, sale, and transportation of intoxicating liquors. Do you know what it *doesn't* prohibit?"

Teddy shook his head.

"It doesn't prohibit the *drinking* of intoxicating liquors."

Teddy's eyes lit up. "In that case . . ."

Jake grinned and poured a fourth glass.

Teddy took the drink Jake offered him and looked around, taking in the room. Along one wall the sideboard sat beneath two large windows that looked out onto Main Street. Two walls contained shelves crammed with law books. The fourth wall contained the chalkboard. A seven-foot-long oak table surrounded by eight chairs took up the middle of the room. One corner held a roll-top desk and a swivel chair, in which Myrtle now sat, eating her pasty.

"I thought it might be a good idea for the four of us to get together to see what we can come up with on this new murder," said Jake. "Sorry George can't be here, but, Teddy, we're glad to have you included. You weren't in on the little confab we had last year when we had a triple murder here in Booker Falls."

"Which Myrtle reminded me did not help us figure out who the real killer was," said Henri.

"Ah, well, yah, that is true," said Jake. "Still, all in all, it might prove helpful in solving *this* case. And, if nothing else, it provides an opportunity for some convivial conversation and the consumption of some fine scotch, eh?"

"Johnny Walker Black Label as I recall," said Myrtle.

"All the way from Scotland," said Jake. "Now," he continued, "shall we start with our suspects? Henri?"

"We have three for sure—" said Henri, "Declan Murphy and his buddy, Noé Vertanen, and Mrs. Redman. Then there are two other possibilities: Mr. Thatcher and his son, Lincoln."

"You consider them suspects?" asked Myrtle.

"Only because they each have a motive—and, at this time at least, a questionable alibi."

"Well, okay, then," said Jake. "Let's put them on the board."

"We should also add Mrs. Redman's brother," said Myrtle. "If Doctor Sherman is correct that it would have taken two people to commit this crime and Mrs. Redman is a suspect, her brother would be her likely accomplice."

"You're right," said Jake. "Do we know what Mrs. Redman's brother's name is?"

"Carl," said Henri. "His first name is Carl. I don't know his last name."

Jake picked up a piece of chalk and wrote across the top of the chalkboard: DECLAN, NOÉ, TALLULAH, CARL,

ORVILLE, and LINCOLN.

"Motives?" said Jake when he finished.

"Under Declan and Tallulah put *revenge*," said Myrtle. "And question marks under Noé and Carl."

"Or just *accomplice*," said Teddy.

Jake wrote down both suggestions.

"And under Orville you could also write *revenge,* and under Lincoln, *money*," said Henri.

"How about alibis?" asked Jake.

"That's easy;" said Teddy, "none, all the way across the board. Nobody had a good alibi."

"For sure, Mrs. Redman's and her brother's, as well as Declan's and Noé's are questionable," said Myrtle. "But I'm still perplexed by the Thatchers."

"What do you mean?" asked Jake.

"They said they had gone to the cabin because of a note they got from Professor Thatcher asking them to meet him there."

"Right," said Henri. "But they probably made up the part about the note."

"That's just it," said Myrtle. "Why would they say it if it weren't true? I mean, all they really had to say was that they had gone there; they wouldn't have had to give a reason unless it was true—unless there really was a note."

"To make it sound more authentic?" said Teddy.

"But did it really?" asked Myrtle. "I'm not sure."

"Nevertheless, that's their alibi, so we'll put it down," said Jake. "Now, how about a murder weapon? Can we connect a murder weapon to any of these people?"

"That's another problem," said Henri, "since we're still not sure exactly what type of weapon was used."

"Except Doctor Sherman doesn't think it was an ordinary knife;" added Myrtle, "which pretty much leaves out the missing knife from the workshop."

"We can't connect anything to Declan except that he might have used a railroad spike," said Henri.

"But we didn't find anything like that at his place," said Teddy.

"True," said Henri.

"We did find those wooden stakes at Noé's, though," said Teddy.

"Stakes?" said Jake.

Henri explained what Noé told him about the stakes: where they came from, what they had been used for, and how he had come by them.

"He says he has a dozen;" added Henri, "but so far we've only found eleven. It's possible the missing one is our murder weapon. Teddy went out to Noé's place today and brought back all of them that were still there, but we're missing one. We dropped them off at Doc Sherman's office for him to test for blood."

"Under Mrs. Redman's name, put knitting needles," said Myrtle.

Jake looked at her, confused. "Needles?"

"Knitting needles," said Myrtle. She went on to describe the needles, how long they might be and their shape. "One of those could also be the murder weapon."

Jake shrugged, and under TALLULAH wrote "needles."

"And the Thatchers?" he asked.

Henri shook his head. "Nothing yet. But we haven't searched their place, either."

"Why not?" asked Jake.

"No probable cause," answered Henri. "I talked to Judge Hurstbourne yesterday, but he said my suspicion wasn't enough to give me a warrant. I'd have to come up with something better."

Jake drew question marks under both Orville's and Lincoln's names.

"Anything else?" he asked. "Any other evidence?"

"Nah," said Henri, shaking his head. "And none of the houses had the kind of clothesline used to tie the professor up with."

"Not much to go on;" said Jake, laying the chalk back on the ledge of the chalkboard. He stepped back and looked at what he'd written down. "For sure not enough to charge anyone."

He walked over to the sideboard, picked up the bottle of scotch and went around, refilling everyone's glass.

"So, where do we go from here?" he asked, once he finished.

No one spoke.

"Then I guess we're adjourned," said Jake. "After we finish our drinks, of course."

CHAPTER EIGHTEEN

"So, did I do it? Did I kill Edwin? I been dyin' ta know," said Tallulah when Henri showed up at her door.

"I'm not ready to arrest you yet," said Henri, smiling. "But the day's not over now, is it?"

It had been four days since the chalkboard meeting in Jake's office. Doctor Sherman had tested all the stakes from Noé's place and found no trace of blood on any of them. Henri was no closer to figuring out who the prime suspect was, let alone ready to arrest anyone.

"Well, do ya got my needles? Dat's what I wanta know," said Tallulah.

"I don't have your needles; still keeping them for evidence. But I have some replacements for you."

Henri reached into the bag he was carrying and brought out four needles, the same sizes as the ones he'd taken from Tallulah five days earlier.

Tallulah took the needles from Henri. It was obvious they weren't new; they had seen a lot of use.

"Where'd these come from?" she asked. "Dey's really old."

"Mrs. Darling," said Henri. "Myrtle told her about us having to take yours and how you needed them for your business. Mrs. Darling had some she was no longer using and is happy to loan them to you until you get yours back—that is, if you *do* get yours back."

"Why wouldn't I get mine back?"

"I doubt they would let you have them in prison," said Henri, "since they would have been the kind of weapon you killed the professor with if we find you did it. They wouldn't want you going around stabbing guards—or other inmates."

Tallulah laughed. "Nah, I reckon not. You tell Mrs. Darling I sure do 'preciate it. And I will get 'em back to her, 'cause *I* know I din't kill Edwin. Ain't no reason I won't get my needles back."

"Okay," said Henri. "You have a good day now."

He started to leave but stopped when Tallulah said, "Hey, Constable, I got sometin' for you."

She hurried back into the house then returned, and held out an envelope.

"I went up to Edwin's place after you left to check on da bees. Dey're okay. While I was dere I went in da workshop—"

"You were in the workshop?" asked Henri. "How did you get in? That's still a crime scene."

"Oh, I din't know dat. Anyways, I got a key; Edwin never asked for it back. So, as I was sayin', I went in da workshop to look around. I saw his clothes was hangin' on da hook on da wall so I took dem back to da house—"

"That should be off limits, too," said Henri, clearly disturbed.

"Well," huffed Tallulah, "if ya don't want people snoopin' 'round, maybe you should put up signs, eh? Now, do ya want dis or not?"

Henri sighed. "Sure, okay. Where did you find it?"

"In his coat pocket. Here."

Henri took the envelope from Tallulah. It was addressed to "Miss Myrtle Tully."

"I'll see that she gets it," said Henri. "Perhaps you and I will speak again."

"Let's not," said Tallulah, slamming the door shut in his face.

*****

Myrtle had decided that, while she enjoyed being picked up after work by either George or Henri, the time had come for her to take the Model N out of the barn. They could still pick her up but on occasion she'd drive herself. She had asked Andy Erickson to come by and inspect her Ford to make sure it was ready to drive.

Today was the first day she was on her own.

She'd closed up the library and was back at the boarding house in less than ten minutes. To her surprise, everyone was just sitting down to dinner.

"Wonderful!" she exclaimed. "I get to eat with all of you. What's for dinner?"

"Meatloaf," said Mrs. Darling setting the platter down on the table. "Boiled potatoes, peas, cottage cheese—"

"Wait," said Daisy. "What kind of cheese?"

"Cottage cheese. Made it myself."

"Let me have a bite," said Henri.

Mrs. Darling spooned out some onto his plate.

He took a bite, then looked up at his landlady. "Mrs. Darling, you are a gift!"

"Okay, okay," said Daisy. "Set it down here so we can all try it."

One by one, Myrtle, Daisy, and Pierre put a portion on their respective plates and took a bite.

"Mrs. Darling, this is delicious!" exclaimed Myrtle. "What's in it?"

"Oh, it's a very involved recipe;" said the old lady, beaming. "Milk, vinegar, and salt."

"That's all?" asked Pierre. "Myrtle's right—this is delicious."

"What about you Daisy?" asked Myrtle. "Do you like it?"

"I'm too busy eating it," said Daisy, pushing another forkful into her mouth, eliciting a laugh from everyone.

"And pecan pie for dessert," said Mrs. Darling, as she retreated to the kitchen.

"You people realize we eat like kings here?" asked Pierre, looking around the table.

"Yeah, Myrtle, you're going to miss all this when you get married and move out," said Daisy as a small boiled potato slipped between her lips. "You're going to have to cook your own dinner."

"First of all," said Myrtle, "what makes you think I'm getting married? Secondly, even if I do, what makes you think I'm moving out. And, third, maybe my husband can cook."

"Can you, Henri?" asked Daisy.

Henri had been too busy eating to pay any attention to the conversation.

"What?" he asked, looking at Daisy. "Did you say something?"

"Daisy asked if you knew how to cook," said Pierre.

All this time a blush was flaring across Myrtle's cheeks.

Henri looked confused. "Do I know how to cook? Why should I?"

Daisy and Pierre broke out laughing.

"Let's talk about something else," said Myrtle, picking up her glass of milk. "Anything new today on the case?" she asked Henri.

"Nah. We're right where we were four days ago. Oh, wait, there is one thing—Mrs. Redman found an envelope in Professor Thatcher's coat, the one hanging in the workshop. It had your name on it."

"An envelope for me?"

"Yah, I'll get it right after dinner and bring it to your room."

*****

Myrtle heard a knock on her door.

As soon as dinner was over she'd headed upstairs. She was anxious to get into the book she'd checked out earlier that day: *The Mysterious Affair at Styles*, by Agatha Christie. It had been published a few years ago, but the library had only recently received a copy.

"Who's there?" Myrtle called out.

"It's Henri," came the voice from the other side of the door. "I have that envelope Mrs. Redman gave me to give to you."

I'd completely forgotten about that, thought Myrtle.

"Come on in," she said. She smoothed back her hair with one hand.

Henri opened the door and walked in. He held out the envelope to Myrtle, and she opened it.

Inside was a second envelope. Myrtle read aloud what was written on it: "Open only in the event of my death. Edwin Thatcher."

Myrtle gave Henri a questioning look. "Is this an April's Fool joke?" she asked.

Henri looked confused. "What do you mean?"

"Today—today is April first, April Fool's Day."

Henri laughed. "I didn't know that. I don't keep up with trivial things like that."

"Oh, I know," said Myrtle, "you're so prim and formal."

A panged look came across Henri's face. "I wouldn't say that," he said.

"I'm sorry; I didn't mean to hurt your feelings. Okay, since the professor *is* dead, let's see what he had to tell me."

She tore open the envelope and removed a single sheet of paper. Again, she read aloud.

I am convinced that my brother, Orville Thatcher, is planning to kill me. In the event of my death, whether by what appears to be natural causes, an accident, or foul play, attention should be given to him. He is angry with me because I did not leave the cabin to him in my will. Edwin Thatcher

Myrtle looked at Henri, her eyes wide. "The professor thought his brother was planning on killing him!"

"And now he's dead," said Henri.

"What do you think? Is it possible?"

"We did put his and Lincoln's name up on the chalkboard."

Henri took a deep breath. "And it appears the professor thought it might happen. First thing tomorrow I'll get a search warrant for the Thatcher place."

CHAPTER NINETEEN

Once Henri showed the note to Judge Hurstbourne, there was no question of obtaining a warrant to search Orville's property.

Henri had considered leaving Teddy at the jail and taking Myrtle with him but then thought better of it. If any evidence was found that called for an immediate arrest, better to have Teddy, an officer of the law who carried a gun rather than a civilian—a woman at that—whose only weapon was a derringer.

He'd also called George to go along, figuring three was better than two since there were two Thatchers.

"Constable, what can I do for you?" asked Orville when he opened the door.

"Mr. Thatcher, I have a warrant to search your property," said Henri, handing the paper to Orville.

"Search my property?" said Orville. "What in da world for?"

Henri ignored Orville's question. "Is Lincoln here?" he asked.

"Yah, he is. Why?"

"I'm going to ask the two of you to step out front with Mr. Salmon while Teddy and I do our search," said Henri.

Orville shrugged, then called Lincoln to come and join him.

"Teddy," said Henri, "you take the shed out back. I'll start in the house. When you're finished come in and join me. Don't forget to wear your gloves," he added, slipping his on.

Ten minutes into his search, Henri heard Teddy enter through the back door.

"Find anything?" Henri asked.

"You might say that," said Teddy, entering the office where Henri was searching. "These."

In one hand he held two objects. One was the missing knife from the set in Edwin's workshop; it had blood on it. The second was a coil of clothesline. To Henri's eye, it looked the same as that used to tie Edwin Thatcher to the chair when he had been stabbed to death.

In his other hand Teddy held a metal cone about twelve inches in length, tapered to a rounded point.

"Does this look like what Doc Sherman said the murder weapon might look like?" he asked.

"It sure does," said Henri. "Let's keep looking here in the house. You take the kitchen."

Continuing his search of the office, Henri opened the bottom drawer of a small writing desk and found an envelope, eight by twelve, with the name and address of the Karhu Insurance Agency, 621 Sibley Avenue, Hancock, Michigan, printed over an outline of a bear. Henri removed two pieces of paper from the envelope. One was a life insurance policy in the amount of ten thousand dollars. The insured's name was Edwin Thatcher. The beneficiary: Orville Thatcher. The second item was a copy of the application signed by Orville Thatcher.

After he finished checking the office but found nothing else of consequence, Henri joined the other four men in the front yard.

"Orville Thatcher, Lincoln Thatcher, you're both under arrest. Teddy, handcuff them."

"Under arrest?" said Lincoln. "What for?"

"For the murder of Edwin Thatcher," said Henri.

"There must be some mistake," said Orville.

"You can explain it to a jury," said Henri.

*****

When they reached the jail, Henri questioned Orville in his office while Teddy, against the protestations of both Declan and Noé, herded them into the same cell, then placed Lincoln into the one now left vacant.

"How do you explain this?" Henri asked, placing the knife on the desk.

"I don't know what you mean," said Orville. "I ain't never seen dat knife before. Is it da one used to kill Edwin?"

"And this?" Henri lay the coil of clothesline on the desk next to the knife.

"It's clothesline. What about it?"

"Is it yours?"

"It looks like mine," said Orville. "But I ain't used it since winter set in. What about it?"

"It's the same kind of clothesline used to tie up your brother."

"I don't know nothin' 'bout dat, neither."

"Right," said Henri. "I suppose you also don't know anything about this."

He laid the policy and the application down in front of Orville.

Orville looked at the two pieces of paper, squinting his eyes as if trying to understand what was happening.

"I ain't never seen neither of dese before, either," he said.

"Is that your signature on the application?" asked Henri.

Orville looked at the application, again squinting.

"Well, yah, it kinda looks like my signature. But I never signed dat paper."

"And how about this?" Henri reached down, pulled out the long metal cone, and laid it on the desk."

"Oh, sure," said Orville, "dat's mine. Dat's my marlinspike."

"A marlinspike, huh? And what do you use a marlinspike for?"

"Oh, lots o' tings. Most every boat's got at least one. You use dem to unlay ropes, untie knots—lots o' tings."

"Is this the only one you have?" asked Henri. "We didn't find any more in the shed."

"Dat's it. Used to have tree or four but when I quit fishin' I only kept dat one."

"How about Lincoln—does he have any?"

"Nah. Used to. Den his boat sank."

By this time Teddy had joined the two men.

"Teddy, please put Mr. Thatcher in the cell and bring Lincoln in here."

*****

Henri got no further with Lincoln than he had with his father.

He had no knowledge of the knife, he said, nor did he know anything about the life insurance policy.

Yes, he knew what a marlinspike was, but, as far as he knew, this one was the only one his father owned.

"What can you tell me about the clothesline?" asked Henri.

Lincoln looked at Henri, confused.

"The clothesline," said Henri. "What do you know about

the clothesline we found in your shed?"

"It's white," said Lincoln, still not comprehending the question. "Or it used to be; kinda gray now from layin' out in da shed all winter. We use it to hang da clothes on in da summer. Not da winter dough—too cold. Dey'd freeze."

Henri grimaced. "I want to know if you were the one who cut off the pieces used to tie up your uncle before you stabbed him to death."

Lincoln sat up straight. Now he knew what Henri was getting at.

"Nah, nah! We never killed him! I don't know nothin' 'bout dat!"

"But you did know you were the sole beneficiary in Professor Thatcher's will?"

"Yah, sure," said Lincoln, relaxing. "I already told you dat."

"Maybe you couldn't wait until the professor died from the cancer. Maybe you needed the money right away, or Joker would make life miserable for you."

"No way. I had a deal wit Joker. I told him I was gettin' Uncle Edwin's money and he agreed to wait if I paid him a extra ten percent."

"And you say you and your father were at the cabin all night, that you never went to your uncle's house?"

"Dat's right."

"Can anyone confirm that? Did anyone see you there?"

Lincoln shook his head. "Nah. We didn't see nobody."

"Teddy, come and take Lincoln back to his cell, will you?" asked Henri.

When Teddy got back to the office, he sank down into the chair Lincoln had just vacated.

"Did you learn anything?" he asked.

"Yah—that we might have one more suspect."

"Oh?"

"Joker Mulhearn," said Henri.

*****

"You found all this in Orville Thatcher's home?" asked Jake.

After Teddy left, Henri had called Jake and told him he thought they'd found out who murdered Edwin Thatcher. He suggested they meet at his office where he had laid out all the evidence and shared with Jake what the two suspects had told him.

"The insurance policy;" said Henri, "the clothesline, the knife, and the marlinspike were in the shed."

"And they both claim to be innocent?"

"Yah, they do."

"And you don't think Joker had anything to do with it?" asked Jake.

"Nah. While I was waiting for you I walked over to the bar. He told me he'd been serving beer all night the evening the professor was killed. And there were a dozen men there who backed him up."

"He could have had someone do it for him."

"I doubt it. Joker's the kind who likes to take care of things personally—doesn't leave any witnesses that way. You know Leonard Wysocki, don't you?"

"With the State Police?"

"Yah, that's him. He's coming tomorrow with a crew to take fingerprints at the professor's house. I'm going to have him take the knife and the clothesline and the marlinspike and the insurance policy and the envelope back with him to see if he can get any prints off of those. I'm also going to send Mrs. Redman's knitting needles and the stakes from Noé's home to have them double checked for blood; you know, just in case. We should know something before the end of the week."

CHAPTER TWENTY

Five days had passed since Orville Thatcher and his son had been arrested. Leonard had arrived on Monday with his crew and, after lifting fingerprints from Professor Thatcher's home, workshop, and the barn, took everything with him back to Marquette along with all the evidence Henri had given him to check.

On Friday he returned to Booker Falls to meet Jake in his office along with Henri, and Myrtle, whom Jake had requested sit in on the meeting.

"First of all," said Leonard, "there was no blood on any of the possible murder weapons, the needles, or any of the stakes or the marlinspike."

"What about the blood on the knife?" asked Jake. "Was it the professor's?"

"It was the same type," said Leonard. "But that's all we can tell; no way to know if it was the deceased's."

"And fingerprints?" asked Henri. "What did you find there?"

"Thanks to your fingerprinting the four suspects you arrested, we had those to compare to any we found. We went on the assumption that the prints on the knitting needles were Mrs. Redman's, since they belonged to her. And we didn't have any for this Carl person.

"The only prints on the three possible murder weapons were those of the people who owned them: Mrs. Redman's on the needles, Noé's on the stakes, and Mr. Thatcher's on the marlinspike. The only ones found at the professor's place were Mrs. Redman's, Lincoln's, and the professor's. There were no fingerprints on the knife. Whoever used it must have wiped it clean."

"But why wouldn't they have wiped the blood off, too?" asked Henri.

Leonard shook his head. "Don't know. Perhaps they were in too much of a hurry. Maybe they just overlooked it. As far as the clothesline goes, it wasn't possible to get any prints from it, but it definitely was the same type found at the crime scene."

"What about the insurance policy?" asked Jake.

"There's where it gets strange," said Leonard. "There was one set of prints on the policy itself as well as on the application and the envelope they were in."

"Orville's?" asked Jake.

"Nah," replied Leonard. "Mr. Karhu—the insurance man who issued the policy. We had his prints on file from his application to sell insurance."

"Wait a minute," said Myrtle. "You're telling us Mr. Thatcher's prints were not on any of those?"

"That's right," said Leonard. "Just one set of prints: Mr. Karhu's."

"How is that possible?" asked Jake. "Wouldn't Orville's prints be all over those items?"

"He definitely signed the application; he confirmed it was his signature," said Henri. "Leonard, is it possible the prints were wiped off like they were with the knife?"

"Our expert says it's almost impossible to wipe prints off of paper because it's so porous," answered Leonard. "The deposit the print leaves sinks right into the paper; not like on the handle of a knife or a gun."

"Myrtle, what do you make of all this?" asked Jake. "You've been pretty quiet."

"Yah," said Henri, "not like you at all."

Myrtle gave him a dirty look. Then she looked at the other men.

"All the evidence certainly seems to point toward Mr. Thatcher and his son," she said. "But, you're right—no prints of Mr. Thatcher's anywhere in the professor's home or workshop or the paperwork.... I just don't know. Then there's the knife—it doesn't match at all the type of weapon Doctor Sherman says was used. And there's one other thing, too."

"What's that?" asked Jake.

"The photographs of the crime scene; there's something wrong there but I can't put my finger on it."

Jake turned to Henri. "Mr. Thatcher confirmed he signed the application?" he asked.

"Yah. But he seemed a bit uncertain of it."

"Would you have Teddy bring him up here? I want to get a sample of his signature."

After a quick phone call to the jail, Teddy appeared with Orville.

"Mr. Thatcher," said Jake, "here's a piece of paper and a pen. Would you sign your name, please?"

"Yah, sure," said Orville, bending down over the table.

"You're left-handed?" asked Myrtle, watching Orville as he wrote his signature.

"Yah, it's a curse——and one I passed on to Lincoln."

"Left-handedness runs in a family. Was your wife left-handed?" asked Myrtle.

"Nah. She was normal, like most people."

"Why did you ask about him being left-handed?" asked Jake after Orville left with Teddy.

"I don't know," said Myrtle. "I don't see that many left-handed people. I'm pretty sure it's a rarity."

Henri had been studying Orville's signature while the conversation was going on. He looked up.

"Sure looks like the same signature to me as on the application," he said.

Jake checked out both pieces of paper. "Yep. You're right. I'm going to see Judge Hurstbourne about setting a court date and getting Mr. Thatcher and his son charged. Do you know if either of them has a lawyer?"

"Mr. Thatcher said he wants Roy Draper to represent both of them," said Henri.

"He's not very experienced," said Jake. "I'm sure he's never had a murder case before."

"Yah," said Henri. "But he's cheap and the Thatchers don't have much money."

CHAPTER TWENTY-ONE

"All rise; the Honorable Clarence Hurstbourne now presiding."

Everyone stood as Judge Hurstbourne entered the courtroom and took his place. When he was seated, he waved his hand and everyone sat down.

Six-foot-four and weighing over two hundred and seventy pounds, Clarence Hurstbourne was an intimidating presence behind the bench. Sixty-one-years-old, he had served as county judge for the past seventeen years, earning a reputation as a firm, but fair, administrator of the law.

The steely eyes that peered out from under a pair of bushy eyebrows were as daunting as they had been forty-three years earlier when he was a starting guard for the first football team ever fielded by the University of Michigan.

"So, what've we got here?" asked the judge, once everyone was seated.

Fred Wilkerson, court bailiff longer than Hurstbourne had been judge, read the charges: "Orville Thatcher—murder in the first degree. Lincoln Thatcher—murder in the first degree."

"Are the accused present?" asked Hurstbourne.

Roy Draper, along with Orville and Lincoln, rose to their feet.

"They are, Your Honor," said Draper. "Roy Draper, for the defense."

"How do your clients plead?" asked Hurstbourne.

"Not guilty, Your Honor," answered Draper.

"Mr. McIntyre, are you ready to make your opening statement?" asked the judge.

"I am, Your Honor."

Jake stood and casually made his way to the jury box where twelve jurors who had been selected the day before sat.

"Gentlemen...ladies," Jake added, nodding to the two women present.

"The state will show that on the twenty-fifth day of March of this year, the two men who stand accused before you did, with malice aforethought, cause the death of one Edwin Thatcher, brother to the accused, Orville Thatcher, and uncle of Lincoln Thatcher; that they came upon the deceased in his workshop, bound him and stabbed him in the heart, causing instant death.

"The state will show how the accused did plan and carry out this heinous crime and will ask you to find them guilty and sentence them both to life imprisonment. Thank you."

The judge looked at Draper. "Mr. Draper?"

"Thank you, Your Honor," said Draper.

"What Mr. McIntyre will *not* show you," he said as he stood and approached the jury, "is the murder weapon that was used or even what type of weapon it was because, 'A,' no weapon has yet been found and, 'B,' the coroner cannot say for sure what the weapon was. What the prosecutor will *not* show you are fingerprints of either of the accused on any key pieces of evidence, because there are none to be found. What he will *not* show you are any witnesses to the crime nor any confessions my clients made—because there are none and they made none.

"*I* will show that on the night in question my clients were out of town, on the Portage River, a good four-hour ride from here by sleigh, and that they spent the night there. I will also show you that there were other suspects in this murder case whom the prosecution chose to ignore. Thank you."

"What do you think?" Daisy whispered to Myrtle.

Myrtle had taken off work to attend the trial. Daisy was covering it for the paper.

"Mr. Thatcher and his son could be in trouble," said Myrtle. "Although Mr. Draper does make some good points."

"Mr. McIntyre, are you ready to call your first witness?" asked Judge Hurstbourne.

"I am, Your Honor. I call to the stand Constable Henri de la Cruz."

Normally, Henri dressed casually: jeans, plaid shirt, and a denim jacket. Today he was in his official attire: his constable's uniform—tan slacks and a jacket buttoned up to his neck. Two hash marks decorated his left sleeve. His hair, usually combed straight back, was parted down the middle.

"Is he the one?" whispered Daisy as Henri was being sworn in, holding her hand over her mouth hoping the judge couldn't hear her.

"The one who?" Myrtle whispered back.

"The lucky guy."

Myrtle smiled. "I told you you'd be the third one to know."

"Ahem."

The two women looked up at Judge Hurstbourne who was giving them the evil eye. They sunk down into their seats.

"Constable," said Jake, "it was you who found Edwin Thatcher's body, is that right?"

"Me and Myrtle Tully," said Henri.

"Can you describe the scene when you arrived?"

Over the next ten minutes, Henri explained how he and Myrtle had found Edwin dead, murdered, in the workshop. That he had called Doctor Sherman to come and to bring Daisy with him and how he and Myrtle had checked out the crime scene, being careful not to disturb anything.

"And then, after the doctor left with the body to take it to his office, what did you do?" asked Jake.

"I made sure the fire was out in the fireplace. While I was waiting for Doc to arrive I called and talked to Mrs. Darling who told me the professor had a brother—Orville. I then called Mr. Littlefield, the mail carrier, and obtained his address.

"Miss Tully and I drove to Mr. Thatcher's home, but no one was there. His neighbor—"

"Mrs. Jones?"

"Yah, that's right, Mrs. Jones. She said she saw Mr. Thatcher and his son leave earlier that day in a sleigh. She said she also had seen someone around the house shortly after they had gone, but didn't know who it was."

"Did she see Mr. Thatcher and his son later that evening?"

"She said she did not."

"And what happened next?"

"I took Miss Tully to my office and left her there while I went looking for Declan Murphy."

"Declan Murphy? Why were you looking for Declan Murphy?"

"At that time, he was a suspect because of previous threats he'd made against Professor Thatcher."

"But you didn't find him?"

"Nah."

"And he's no longer a suspect?"

"Nah."

"Then what happened?" asked Jake.

"I picked Myrtle up at my office and we went back to the boarding house."

"You continued your investigation the next day?"

"Yah. The next morning Miss Tully and I again went to Mr. Thatcher's home but found no one there. Mrs. Jones said she hadn't seen either of them. We then went to Professor Thatcher's home where we collected evidence from the workshop, then went into the barn."

"The evidence you took included pieces of clothesline?"

"Yah, they were what the professor had been tied up with."

"Your Honor, the prosecution would like to enter these four pieces of clothesline as prosecution exhibit 'A'," said Jake. "Now, Constable, did you find similar clothesline in the house, the workshop, or the barn?"

"Nah."

"Then the murderer must have brought the clothesline with him—which indicates this crime was one of premeditation."

"Objection," said Draper.

"On what grounds?" asked Judge Hurstbourne.

"Two, Your Honor," said Draper. "First of all, we don't know if the killer was a man or a woman. I'm under the impression that in addition to Mr. Thatcher and Lincoln and this Murphy fellow there was initially another suspect, a female. Second, the absence of the remaining clothesline could be attributed to the possibility the murderer took it with him—or her—but that it was originally at the deceased's home, which would not indicate premeditation."

"Right on both counts," said the judge. "The jury will keep in mind that the sex of the perpetrator has not yet been determined and that the absence of the remaining clothesline on the victim's property does not prove premeditation. Mr.

McIntyre, you may proceed."

"That was a pretty smart catch," whispered Daisy.

"Yes, it was," replied Myrtle.

"All right, now, Constable you didn't find the murder weapon."

"Nah, no murder weapon. We did find a set of knives and one was missing."

"So that knife could have been the murder weapon," said Jake.

"Objection," said Draper, getting to his feet. "Calls for speculation."

"Sustained," said Hurstbourne.

"Your Honor," said Jake, "I'm not asking the constable if he *thought* the knife was the murder weapon, only if it could have been."

Judge Hurstbourne thought for a moment, then said, "You're right. Objection overruled. The witness may answer."

"I guess it *could* have been," said Henri, "although Doc Sherman doesn't think so."

"All right. Did you find anything in the barn?" asked Jake.

"Yah, bees."

"Bees?"

"Yah. The professor kept bees—for the honey and the beeswax."

"That's all you found?"

"In the barn, yah; no more evidence. Then we searched the house."

"And what did you find there?"

"We found the professor's will."

"Your Honor, we enter as exhibit 'B' for the prosecution, this will, dated the seventh of February of this year.

"Constable, did you read the will?"

"I did."

"And?"

"The professor left everything to Lincoln Thatcher—his nephew."

"Was anything else found in the house relative to the case?"

"No more evidence," said Henri. "But Miss Tully did find a bottle of morphine."

"Do you know why Professor Thatcher was taking morphine?"

"Doc Sherman said his autopsy showed the professor was suffering from cancer."

Jake removed a handkerchief from his pocket and mopped his forehead. The room wasn't particularly hot but, bearing the weight he did, he was sweating profusely.

"What happened then?" asked Jake.

"After we left the professor's home, Miss Tully and I returned to my office where I received a phone call from my deputy, Teddy Simpson, saying that he had located Declan Murphy. I went and joined Teddy and we arrested Declan and another man who was with him, Noé Vertanen. We arrested them for public drunkenness and took them back to the jail."

"At that time you still considered Mr. Murphy a suspect?"

"And maybe Noé, too."

"Why him?"

"Doc Sherman said he thought there might have been two men involved in the murder."

"Objection, your honor."

Judge Hurstbourne looked at Draper. "Objection? On what grounds?"

"Again, Constable de la Cruz has referred to the murderer —or murderers—as being male. Your honor has already ruled that we don't know that for sure."

"Constable de la Cruz did not say the perpetrators were

male," said Jake. "He is merely repeating what Doctor Sherman said."

"He's right, Mr. Draper. Objection overruled. And don't even think about objecting for hearsay; Doc Sherman is scheduled to be one of the witnesses. But, again, I remind the jury that it is unknown if the murderer or murderers were male or female."

Jake turned to Henri. "What happened then?"

"I phoned Judge Hurstbourne to get warrants to search their houses," said Henri. "I left Teddy at the jail to wait for them while Miss Tully and I took another run at Mr. Thatcher's home."

"And was he home this time?" asked Jake.

"Yah, he was. He said he and Lincoln spent the night at a cabin over by the Portage River, that he'd gotten a note from Professor Thatcher to meet him there."

"And did Mr. Thatcher produce the note?"

"Nah. Said he got angry when his brother didn't show up and threw it in the fire."

"And can anyone confirm the two spent the night at the cabin that night?"

"I didn't ask then because they weren't suspects at that time. Later on, after I arrested them, I asked them and they said no, there was no one to confirm it."

"Did any other pertinent information come out of that meeting?" asked Jake.

"At the time, nothing that seemed relevant. But looking back, I see that Mr. Thatcher was angry with his brother about the whole cabin situation and Lincoln being the professor's sole beneficiary, so he had that motive. Plus, he was in debt to Joker Mulhearn, who was pressing him for the money. When I first met Lincoln he had a black eye. I suspect Joker gave it to him."

"Objection, Your Honor, shows facts not in evidence."

"Objection sustained."

"Constable," said Jake, "how do you know Lincoln Thatcher owed money to Joker and that Joker was pressing him for it?"

"He told me."

"*Who* told you?" asked Jake, "Lincoln or Joker?"

"Lincoln."

"Was anything else discussed?"

"Nothing that pertained to the case. Oh, wait—there was one more thing. Lincoln said Professor Thatcher had been engaged but had broken it off, and that his fiancé was very angry and had threatened the professor."

"This was Mrs. Redman?"

"Yah, that's right. So after Miss Tully and I left the Thatcher's, we stopped by Doc Sherman's office to get the results of the autopsy and then drove on over to Mrs. Redman's home, where I interviewed her."

"I don't know why he keeps saying *he* did all the interviews," Myrtle whispered to Daisy. "I was right there. I asked questions, too."

"I'm guessing it's because officially you shouldn't have been there," Daisy whispered back.

"Yeah, maybe so," said Myrtle. "But I was still there."

"Was Mrs. Redman considered a suspect at that point?" asked Jake.

"In the beginning, yes, but once it became clear Mr. Thatcher and his son were the most likely suspects, she no longer was."

"Now when and how did Mr. Thatcher and Lincoln become your primary suspects?"

"On my second trip to Mrs. Redman's home to drop off some knitting needles that Mrs. Darling gave me to loan Mrs.

Redman, she gave me an envelope she said she'd found in a pocket of Professor Thatcher's coat. It was hanging in the workshop the night he was killed."

"You had not searched the coat?" asked Jake.

Henri looked a little flushed. "Nah, didn't seem to be any reason to."

"And what was in the envelope?"

"On the outside, it was addressed to Miss Myrtle Tully."

"You delivered the envelope to Miss Tully?"

"I did."

"And do you know what was in the envelope?"

"Yah, a note written by Professor Thatcher. Myrtle read it to me."

Jake walked back to his desk, picked up the note, walked back to Henri and handed it to him.

"Constable, please read out loud what the note says."

Henri took the note and read it.

Jake took the note back. "Your Honor, I'd like to submit this as exhibit 'C'."

Judge Hurstbourne nodded.

"What happened then, Constable?" asked Jake.

"I got a warrant from the Judge to search Mr. Thatcher's property. Teddy and I went to the Thatcher home and executed it."

"And what did you find?"

"Five items: an insurance policy purchased by Mr. Thatcher on his brother in the amount of ten thousand dollars; a copy of the application for the policy; the missing knife from the set found at the murder scene; and a coil of clothesline."

"Did the knife have blood on it?"

"Yah, it did."

"And was the blood the same type as Professor

Thatcher's?"

"Yah, the blood type was the same but as I said—"

"Thank you, Henri;" Jake interrupted, "and was the clothesline the same as that used to bind Professor Thatcher?"

"Yah, it was."

"Your Honor," said Jake, "I offer into evidence these four items as prosecution exhibits 'D', 'E', 'F', and 'G'."

"What did you do then?" he asked, turning back to Henri.

"I arrested Mr. Thatcher and Lincoln and Teddy and I escorted them to jail."

"And did you interview Mr. Thatcher there?"

"I did. He denied any knowledge of any of the items—except the clothesline. He said it was his."

"And did you interview Lincoln?"

"I did. But he was no more forthcoming than his father. I asked him if anyone could confirm that he and Mr. Thatcher spent the night at the cabin; he said no. He did admit he knew he was the beneficiary of Professor Thatcher's will."

"Constable, was any attempt made to determine if this murder might have been perpetrated in the commission of a robbery?" asked Jake.

"Yah. The night Miss Tully and I found the professor, I looked around his house and didn't see anything out of order. Of course, I'd never been in the house before so I couldn't be sure nothing had been taken. Later on, Mrs. Redman accompanied me and confirmed that everything was still there."

"And you took her because . . . ?"

"She and the professor had been engaged and she had spent time in his home. I thought she would know if something was missing."

"And this took place after Mrs. Redman had been cleared as a suspect?"

"Yah, that's right," said Henri.

"Thank you, Constable. No further questions."

Judge Hurstbourne looked up at the Giltwood clock hanging on the back wall.

"Mr. Draper, before you begin your questioning of Mr. de la Cruz, we will take a fifteen-minute break. Court adjourned until eleven o'clock."

CHAPTER TWENTY-TWO

"Are you nervous about being called as a witness?" asked Daisy.

She and Myrtle were out in the hallway waiting for the trial to reconvene.

"No, not really—you?"

"To tell you the truth—yeah. I'm not much of a public speaker."

"All you have to do is answer their questions about the photos," said Myrtle. "Nothing to it."

"I hope not. You know, Henri said he and Teddy found five pieces of evidence at the Thatcher's. But I only heard him mention four."

"The fifth was the marlinspike. It could have been the murder weapon. But I understand from Henri that Mr. Draper persuaded the judge to prevent Mr. McIntyre from introducing it as evidence."

"Really? Why?"

"Because it couldn't be identified as the actual murder weapon."

"Don't you think the jurors might wonder like I did why

Henri only talked about four things when he said there were five?"

Myrtle winked and smiled. "I have a feeling Henri knew exactly what he was saying."

Back in the courtroom, Henri had taken his place in the witness box and Draper was ready to begin his questioning.

"Constable, I want to remind you that you are still under oath," said Judge Hurstbourne.

"Constable de la Cruz," said Draper, "why did you so quickly give up on suspecting either Declan Murphy or Mrs. Redman? And why did you suspect them in the first place?"

"We dismissed them as suspects first of all because of the overwhelming evidence against both Mr. Thatcher and his son. Plus, none of the items we found at Declan's or Noé's or Mrs. Redman's knitting needles appeared to be the murder weapon," said Henri.

"You say 'appeared to be.' But the murder weapon has not yet been recovered, has it?" asked Draper. "Yet the weapon you took from Mr. Thatcher's home was a knife. You said and the coroner confirmed the wound looked more like it might have come from a railroad spike. Now when you located Mr. Murphy the morning after the murder you found him at the railroad depot. Would train tracks be a likely place for one to find a railroad spike?"

"I suppose so," said Henri. "But we didn't find one at Murphy's home."

"Possibly because the reason he and Vertanen were at the depot was to dispose of it somewhere on the tracks," said Draper.

"Objection," said Jake, "calls for speculation—on the part of Mr. Draper, since he seems to be testifying rather than asking a question."

"Sustained," said the judge.

"All right," said Draper. "Now, from the description of the wound in the coroner's report, it appears that an instrument similar to a knitting needle could have been used."

"Objection, again," said Jake, struggling to get to his feet.

"Nope," said the judge, "this time I've got to overrule you. I saw the report: I agree with Mr. Draper. But make it a question, Mr. Draper, not a statement."

Jake sank down into his chair.

"Yes, Your Honor," said Draper. "I'll address that question later to Doctor Sherman. Now, the Thatchers do not seem to have solid alibis. How about Mr. Murphy and Mrs. Redman? Are their alibis any more solid?"

"No, sir, they are not," said Henri. "No one can corroborate either one of their alibis. Okay, that's not quite correct. Mrs. Redman said she spent the evening with her brother, and Declan claims to have been with Noé."

"But according to Doctor Sherman, it appears there must have been two people involved in Professor Thatcher's murder. So, either Mrs. Redman's brother or Mr. Murphy's friend could be that second person?"

"Objection," said Jake. "Calls for speculation."

"Quite right," said Judge Hurstbourne. "The witness will not answer."

"You see what he's doing?" whispered Myrtle to Daisy. "He's trying to plant reasonable doubt—suggesting Murphy and Mrs. Redman should still be suspects."

"One final question, Constable," said Draper. "Did Mr. Thatcher deny knowledge of any of the evidence found at his home?"

"Yah, said he never saw the knife before, or the insurance policy. Said the clothesline was his."

"Did he confirm that the signature on the application for the policy was his?" asked Draper.

"He did," answered Henri.

"Right off the bat? Like, oh yah, that's my signature all right?"

"Well, nah. He said it looked *kind of* like his signature."

"*Kind of like* his signature? How confident were you that Mr. Thatcher knew for a fact that was his signature?"

"Objection," said Jake. "Calls for speculation."

"Your Honor," said Draper, "I'm not asking the constable if the signature was genuine or even to speculate whether or not it *is* genuine, but merely how confident he was about it."

"Sounds like speculation to me," said Jake. "But in any case, the witness is not a handwriting expert, so I maintain my objection."

"Got to agree with the prosecution on that second point," said the judge. "Objection is sustained."

"No more questions," said Draper as he walked back to his desk.

"Redirect, Your Honor?" asked Jake.

Judge Hurstbourne nodded.

"Henri," said Jake, still standing behind his desk, "you said earlier in your testimony that you recovered five items in your search of the Thatcher's residence."

Draper jumped to his feet, nearly knocking the table over.

"Your Honor, I must object. Sidebar?"

The judge motioned for him and Jake to approach the bench.

"Your Honor has already ruled out any mention of the marlinspike since it has not been proven exactly what the murder weapon was," said Draper in a hushed voice.

"The defense opened the door;" said Jake, "in fact, more than once. He began by asking Henri what made him suspect Declan and Mrs. Redman, which brought up the knitting needles. Then he himself asked about a railroad spike. There is now no reason why I can't inquire about the marlinspike."

"I think he's got you there, Mr. Draper," said Judge Hurstbourne, a slight grin on his face, unlike Draper's expression which was one of distress. "The question of the marlinspike is back in. Step back, gentlemen."

"That being the case," said Jake, "I now ask that the marlinspike be entered as prosecution exhibit 'H'."

"Noted," said the judge. "Now step back.

"Ladies and gentlemen of the jury, an additional piece of evidence is being introduced by the prosecution—a marlinspike found at the home of the defendants. It will be entered as prosecution exhibit 'H.' Mr. McIntyre, you may continue."

"Now, Constable," said Jake, "did Mr. Thatcher or his son —either of them—admit that this marlinspike belonged to them?"

"Mr. Thatcher said it was his, from when he was a fisherman."

"Thank you," said Jake. "No further questions for this witness. The prosecution calls Miss Myrtle Tully."

"Miss Tully," said Jake, once Myrtle had been sworn in and taken her seat, "you were with Constable de la Cruz the evening he found Professor Thatcher's body, is that correct?"

"It is," said Myrtle.

"And how did it happen that the two of you had gone to the Professor's home? Why were you there?"

"Professor Thatcher had been in the library that morning to pick up a book. He asked me to stop by his home when I left work; said he wanted to show me how he made his candles and that he had some honey to give me."

"He was expecting you?" asked Jake.

"Yes," said Myrtle, "which is why I was surprised at how he was dressed."

"How's that?"

"He was only wearing long johns and slippers. I know he wouldn't have greeted me dressed like that."

"And it was that same morning that Professor Thatcher had invited you?"

"Yes."

"We have heard Constable de la Cruz's description of the crime scene. Is there anything you can add?" asked Jake.

"The room was extremely hot when we entered it; there was a huge fire in the fireplace. Professor Thatcher had laid out all of his candle-making equipment on the counter to make candles. Daisy took pictures of all of it."

"Miss O'Hearn?"

"Yes, that's right."

"Anything else?"

"No, I believe Constable de la Cruz covered it quite nicely."

"Miss Tully, you were also with Constable de la Cruz when he found Mr. Thatcher at home the day after the murder, weren't you?"

"I was."

"And did you find it odd that Professor Thatcher would have sent a note to his brother to meet at a cabin forty miles away from town when he was expecting you at his home?"

"I did. I thought it very odd."

"What conclusion did you draw from that?"

"Objection," said Draper. "Calls for speculation."

"Sustained," said Judge Hurstbourne.

"Miss Tully, is there anything else you can add other than what Constable de la Cruz has told the court?" asked Jake.

Myrtle thought for a minute. "Just one thing. When I was studying the photographs of the crime scene something seemed off to me."

"Can you tell us what it was?"

Myrtle shook her head. "No, I've been racking my brain but I can't put my finger on it."

"I have no more questions for this witness," said Jake.

"No questions," said Draper.

"The prosecution calls Doctor Ambrose Sherman," said Jake.

Myrtle took her seat as Dr. Sherman was sworn in.

"Nice job," Daisy whispered.

"I still wish I knew what it was that bothers me about those photos," said Myrtle.

The two of them settled back in their chairs and listened while Doctor Sherman gave his testimony: the cause of death; why he thought more than one perpetrator was involved; that Edwin had cancer; that no drugs were found in his body except for morphine; and the approximate time of death—five-thirty p.m.

"And what about the weapon, Doctor?" asked Jake.

"It did not appear to be a knife, at least not any kind of regular knife. The wound was more circular."

"Would something like this cause such a wound?" asked Jake. He walked back to his desk and held up the marlinspike.

"Objection," said Draper, "calls for speculation."

"Doctor Sherman is familiar with wounds," said Jake, "seeing as how he is also the county coroner. And he has examined the wound sustained by the victim."

"Overruled," said the judge. "The witness may answer."

"Yah," said Doctor Sherman, "something like that could cause such a wound."

"Your report also shows a cut on the deceased's arm. Can you determine what type of weapon was used there?"

"It appeared to have been done with a knife."

"A knife, you say?" said Jake. "A regular knife? And was

that wound inflicted while the deceased was resisting his attackers?"

"Yah, it was a regular knife. And, yah, I think it occurred during the attack."

Jake held up the knife taken from Orville's shed. "This kind of knife?"

"That could do it."

"No further questions," said Jake.

"Doctor Sherman," said Draper getting up, "Mr. McIntyre asked Constable de la Cruz if the blood on the knife was the same type as the victim's, which he confirmed. I put this question to you now—was the blood on the knife that of Professor Thatcher?"

"The blood on the knife was Type A, the same as the deceased's. However, it is not possible to determine if it is Professor Thatcher's blood."

"And approximately what percentage of the population has type A blood, Doctor?"

"About one out of every three."

"In other words, several hundred people right here in Booker Falls have that blood type."

"Yah, that is correct."

"Maybe a third of the people sitting in this courtroom today?"

"It's possible," said Doctor Sherman.

"Now, when Mr. McIntyre suggested the murder weapon appeared to be something like a marlinspike you said it *could* be."

"Yah, that's right."

"But can you say for sure what it *wasn't*?"

"Well, yah, I can say for sure it wasn't a baseball bat, or a bread toaster, or a—"

The room erupted in laughter.

A chagrinned Draper quickly jumped in. "Right, it would not have been any of those. But doctor, *could* it have been one of the knitting needles taken from Mrs. Redman's home? Is that a possibility?"

Doctor Sherman inhaled sharply in exasperation. "Yah, I suppose you could say it was possible but—"

"And *could* it have been one of the stakes taken from Mr. Vertanen's home?"

"That's not as likely but . . . well, yah, I guess it's possible. But—"

"Thank you; no more questions," said Draper, cutting the doctor off.

"Doc, you may be excused," said Judge Hurstbourne. "Gentlemen—and ladies—as illuminating as this is, I think we have heard enough for today."

He turned to the jury.

"Members of the jury, you may go back to your homes for the night. I instruct you not to discuss with each other or with anyone for that matter anything that relates to this trial."

He picked up his gavel and banged it on the desk.

"Court adjourned until ten o'clock tomorrow morning."

CHAPTER TWENTY-THREE

When Mr. Pfrommer was still alive, dinner at the boarding house was always served at precisely five o'clock which precluded Myrtle, except on rare occasions, from dining with her housemates, since she didn't leave the library until six.

Mrs. Darling always made sure a plate was kept warm for her on the big wood-burning iron stove in the kitchen, but Myrtle missed the camaraderie.

After Mr. Pfrommer left for prison, the timing became somewhat more flexible but dinner was still usually finished before Myrtle arrived home.

Since the trial was adjourned for the day and Lydia had offered to close the library, tonight was one of those rare times when Myrtle was able to dine with Henri, Daisy, and Pierre.

"How is the trial going?" asked Pierre, as he cut a slice of ham. He had had classes that day and had not been able to attend.

"I thought Jake did a good job of putting forth the evidence," said Henri.

"I thought Mr. Draper did a good job of introducing

reasonable doubt," said Myrtle.

"What do you mean?" asked Henri.

"You were there," said Myrtle. "Didn't you catch it?"

"I don't know what you're talking about," said Henri.

Myrtle laid down her knife and fork, picked up her napkin, and wiped her lips.

"Okay, here's what I'm talking about. Right off the bat, Mr. Draper made it clear the murderer could have been male or female."

"What do you mean 'right off the bat'?" asked Pierre.

"It's an expression," said Myrtle. "It means it's obvious he was referring to Mrs. Redman. He also brought Declan Murphy back in as a suspect. And there's the whole question of the murder weapon. It hasn't been found yet. It doesn't seem to have been the knife found at Mr. Thatcher's home. In questioning Doctor Sherman, Mr. Draper managed to get in that it was a possibility that either a knitting needle or one of the stakes *could* be the murder weapon. He showed that while the blood on the knife was the same type as Professor Thatcher's, hundreds of other people have that type.

"And finally he pointed out that while the Thatchers couldn't prove their alibis, neither could Mr. Murphy or Mrs. Redman, unless you took the word of his friend and her brother, but then either of them could also be the second perpetrator, the accomplice Doctor Sherman believes was involved. You add it all up and there's a lot of reasonable doubt there."

For a moment no one spoke. Finally, Pierre broke the silence.

"Wow! You were really listening, weren't you?"

"Every word," said Myrtle. She picked up her fork, then laid it down again. "I will say this, though, Henri. That was clever how you and Mr. McIntyre managed to get the marlinspike entered into the conversation and claim it as evidence."

Henri grinned. "That was good, wasn't it? Jake and I talked about how we would do it and it worked out perfectly. We just needed to let Draper open the door for us."

"That's right," said Daisy. "I thought Mr. McIntyre would object when Mr. Draper first brought up the subject of a murder weapon, but he didn't say anything."

"No, he knew if he let Draper bring it up he could get the marlinspike in," said Henri.

"I do have one more observation," said Myrtle. "I'm beginning to suspect someone is trying to frame the Thatchers."

"What makes you think that?" asked Pierre.

"It's all too neat," answered Myrtle. "If they did kill Professor Thatcher wouldn't they have been smart enough to get rid of the evidence—the insurance policy, the clothesline, even the knife?"

"There's no law that says criminals have to be smart," said Pierre.

There was a long silence, finally broken by Daisy.

"Henri, do you know who they're calling as witnesses tomorrow. Will I be one?"

"I think you'll be the first one up," said Henri.

A shocked look came over Daisy's face. "Me? First?"

"Somebody has to be," said Pierre. "Besides, that way you'll get it over and you can relax the rest of the day."

"Maybe you're right," said Daisy. "Who else will be called?"

"I know Jake plans on calling Teddy and Joker and Mrs. Jones," Henri responded. "I don't know who Mr. Draper is calling unless he puts Mr. Thatcher and Lincoln on the stand."

Myrtle had been watching Mrs. Darling as she was serving

while the conversation was going on. She appeared withdrawn, not her usual chatty self.

"Mrs. Darling, are you all right?" she asked.

"Oh, yah," replied the old lady without looking at Myrtle.

"Is something bothering you?" asked Myrtle.

Mrs. Darling shook her head and headed back to the kitchen.

"Do any of you know if something is bothering Mrs. Darling?" asked Myrtle, looking around at the other boarders.

Henri shrugged.

Pierre shook his head.

"Not me," said Daisy. "Why—you think something is?"

"She seemed a little out of sorts," said Myrtle. "Maybe it's just my imagination."

She picked up her fork and took a bite of the slice of apple pie Mrs. Darling had placed in front of her minutes earlier.

*****

Later that evening Myrtle was on her way to the kitchen to make some tea when she heard crying coming from her landlady's room.

She hesitated, wondering if she should intervene.

Yes, she decided, *she would do the same for me.*

She knocked lightly on the closed door.

"Mrs. Darling?" she said softly.

There was no answer for a minute.

Then Mrs. Darling asked, "Who is it?"

"It's Myrtle, Mrs. Darling. I don't mean to interfere but I heard crying coming from your room. Are you all right?"

She heard the old lady shuffling toward the door.

When she opened it, Myrtle's suspicions proved correct. She *was* crying.

"Mrs. Darling, what's wrong? Can I help?"

"Ain't nothin'. I'm just feelin' sad."

"Sad? Sad about what?" asked Myrtle.

Mrs. Darling looked up. "Come on in," she said.

Myrtle walked in and looked around. In the two and a half years she'd been at the boarding house she had never been in Mrs. Darling's room and, in fact, had never seen the inside of it. The door from the hallway had always been closed. It was a big room, at least half again as large as any of the four bedrooms upstairs.

A double bed covered by a flowered-patterned quilt occupied one corner. Both the head and footboards contained patterns with hand-carved symbols. A dresser with a bevel plate mirror stood against one wall. Another wall held a washstand with a towel rack and a marble top holding a blue and white pitcher and bowl with a chinoiserie pattern. On either side of it were a commode and a toilet airer.

Across the room a wardrobe some eight feet in height with a plate glass door took up most of the wall. A third wall held a pedestal cupboard. A chair sat next to it.

A large rocker with an upholstered back and seat to which Mrs. Darling had by now retreated completed the furnishings. All the furniture was oak except for the rocker, which was mahogany.

"May I?" asked Myrtle, pointing to the other chair.

"Yah," said Mrs. Darling.

Myrtle picked the chair up and moved it next to the rocker.

"Now," she said, sitting down and taking her landlady's hand in her own, "tell me what is making you so sad."

"Today would have been my Eugene's eightieth birthday."

"Your late husband?"

"Yah."

"I can understand why you're sad. I know I miss my parents terribly. You don't talk about him much; in fact, I think the only time I ever heard you mention him was the time you got his gun out…oh, and last Christmas, you told us the piano had been his."

"Yah, he was a good piano player, dat one." A smile came to Mrs. Darling's lips as she remembered her husband's playing. "He liked to play hymns. But he also played a lot of music he picked up in da war."

"The Civil War."

"Yah, he fought in it, you know."

"I remember you mentioning that," said Myrtle.

Mrs. Darling had quit crying now. She sat, staring off at nothing.

"Tell me more about him, Mrs. Darling," said Myrtle. "What was he like?"

"He was a good man, a kind man. Me and him, we was married when I was just fifteen. He was twenty-tree. The war was over and he'd just come back to Booker Falls. I'd knowed him before he left but he din't know me—too much difference in our ages, you know. At least I tought he didn't know me.

"But his family lived down the road from our farm and one day he come by to talk wit my father. Said he needed a wife and he tought I would do just fine. My father said he didn't know if he could spare me or not, since I was an only child and dere was a lot of work to do on da farm. Eugene said he had some money saved up from da army and if my father let me marry him he'd buy him a new mule and a new Norfolk plough wit wheels. My father tought dat sounded like a good deal. Me and Eugene was married one week later."

Myrtle was shocked. *Mrs. Darling had been purchased by Mr. Darling to be his wife?*

"I can see you tink it odd how I come to be Mrs. Darling," said Mrs. Darling.

"Well, I…"

"Oh, I din't mind at all. Like I said, I knowed Eugene before he'd went in da army. I mean, I din't know him, but I'd seen him around. I was quite smitten, troot be told. I was happy to be married to him 'cause I din't have to do farming no more."

Myrtle smiled. "That's good. What did Mr. Darling do for a living?"

"He was a gold prospector."

"A gold prospector?"

"Yah, and a good one he was, too. 'Course, we had to have some income 'til he made enough so I went to work at one of da loggin' camps, cookin'."

"Is that how you became such a good cook?" asked Myrtle.

"Oh, no, dearie, I learned to cook in my mama's kitchen. She was a wonderful cook and she taught me everyting I know."

"And when did your husband die?"

Mrs. Darling got a sad look on her face.

"Eighteen-eighty-five—cholera. We was only married twenty years; da best twenty years of my life."

"How did you come to own the boarding house?"

"Eugene, he was a pretty good prospector—took a lot of gold out of da ground. When he died he left me 'nough money to buy dis place and turn it into da boarding house."

Myrtle looked up at the dresser where two photographs sat. She got up and walked over to study them more closely. One was a wedding picture, the other a young boy about five years of age.

"Is this your wedding picture?" she asked.

"Yah, dat's da only one I got of Eugene. Only one of me, too, 'til Daisy started takin' pitchers wit her camera."

"Mr. Darling certainly was attractive;" said Myrtle, "as were you."

"You wouldn't know it to look at me now, but I weren't half-bad lookin' back in dose days."

"And the little boy—who is he?"

Mrs. Darling got to her feet and walked over to Myrtle's side. "Dat's Warren—my little boy."

Myrtle looked at Mrs. Darling. "You have a son?"

"I did; he died a year after dat pitcher was taken. Got cholera, just like his daddy."

"Oh, I'm so sorry."

Myrtle put her arm around Mrs. Darling. "I'm so sorry," she said again.

Mrs. Darling nodded. "Yah, I never got to see him grow up."

Myrtle set the photograph down, turned, and hugged Mrs. Darling.

"I can see why you're so sad," she said.

"I feel better now dat you and me talked. In fact, I tink I'm gonna make some tea. You want some tea?"

"Good! I was on my way to make some when I heard you crying and came in."

"And I'm glad you did," said Mrs. Darling, taking Myrtle's hand and leading her toward the door.

CHAPTER TWENTY-FOUR

Daisy wasn't nearly as nervous as she thought she would be.

After all, for six years after fleeing Chicago and landing in Traverse City, Michigan, she had lived in fear that the family of the husband she thought she had stabbed to death was looking for her, seeking retribution.

She'd changed her name and then, four years ago, when she thought she saw her husband's brother there on the street, moved to Booker Falls.

It was not until the brother showed up and told her that her husband had survived the attack only to die a few years later in a construction accident that she found out what had really happened. But before he died he made him promise that if he ever found Daisy, to let her know he forgave her and it was all his fault.

No, testifying before a bunch of people was not going to be any problem.

"Do you promise to tell the truth, the whole truth, and nothing but the truth so help you God?" asked Teddy Wilkerson, the bailiff.

"I do," said Daisy.

"Miss O'Hearn," said Jake, "you were present at the scene of the crime?"

"I was. I went there with Doctor Sherman."

"And you took pictures of the crime scene?"

"Yes."

"How many pictures did you take?"

"Fourteen."

"And afterward you developed them and turned them over to Constable de la Cruz."

"Yes."

"All of the pictures?"

Daisy looked confused. "Yah. Why wouldn't I?"

"No more questions," said Jake, turning it over to the defense attorney.

"No questions, Your Honor," said Draper, standing and then immediately sitting back down.

"Miss O'Hearn, you are excused," said Judge Hurstbourne.

Daisy looked around. *That's it?*

"Miss O'Hearn, you may step down," the judge said.

Daisy shrugged, stepped out of the witness box, and walked back to her seat next to Myrtle.

"That wasn't so bad, was it?" whispered Myrtle.

"Makes me wonder why I even bothered," said Daisy, obviously disappointed.

"The state calls Teddy Simpson," said Jake.

"Deputy Simpson," said Jake after Teddy had been sworn in, "you were involved in the search of the defendant's property?"

"I was," said Teddy.

"And what did you find?"

"In the shed behind the house I found a coil of clothesline and a knife with what appeared to be blood on it. I also found the marlinspike."

"No further questions," said Jake.

"Deputy," said Draper, "when you found these items, were they hidden from view, covered up?"

"No, they were right there in plain sight."

"You say the knife had blood on it?"

"Just a small amount."

"Thank you. No more questions."

Joker Mulhearn was Jake's next witness.

"Mr. Mulhearn, what is your occupation?" asked Jake.

"You mean, how do I make a livin'?"

"Yes, that is what I mean."

Joker's answer elicited a chorus of loud laughter from spectators. Even Judge Hurstbourne allowed a smile to cross his face.

"I work as a custodian for Alton Woodruff at his barbershop."

"A custodian you say," said Jake.

"Yah—a custodian."

"Mr. Mulhearn, do you also supplement your income by sometimes loaning money to people in need?"

Joker grinned. "Oh, yah, I do. I like to help out where I can."

"And did you loan money to Lincoln Thatcher?" asked Jake.

"Yah, sure. I loaned Lincoln money to buy his boat."

"And what happened to the boat?"

"It sunk."

"It sunk?"

"Yah, you know, like to da bottom o' da lake—it sunk."

"Did Lincoln Thatcher ever repay you the money you loaned him?"

"Nah, not yet." Joker looked menacingly at Lincoln. "But

he will."

"How do you ensure your debtors repay you? What is your method of collecting these debts?"

"First off I try to be nice," said Joker. "But sometimes if dat don't work I use other methods."

"Was the black eye Constable de la Cruz noticed Lincoln was wearing when he first met him a result of your collection methods?"

"As I recall, when Lincoln and I was discussin' repayment he tripped and fell into da door."

"Tripped and fell into the door, eh?" said Jake.

"As I recall, yah."

"Thank you, Mr. Mulhearn, no more questions."

"Mr. Mulhearn," said Draper, "did you make an arrangement with Lincoln Thatcher to extend the date by which the loan had to be repaid?"

"Yah…for a slight consideration."

"He agreed to pay you an extra ten percent?" asked Draper.

"Yah, dat's right—ten percent."

"And how much extra time did you allow Mr. Thatcher to pay you back?"

"Until his uncle kicked da bucket. He was dyin', ya know."

"Yes, we do know that. Thank you, Mr. Mulhearn. I have no more questions for this witness."

"Your Honor, I have one more witness," said Jake. "I call to the stand Paul Momet."

Judge Hurstbourne chuckled. "Paul Momet, eh? Did you have to subpoena him?"

Jake smiled, remembering his previous encounter with Paul Momet. "No, Your Honor, he came willingly."

Once Momet was sworn in, Judge Hurstbourne said, "It's

good to see you back in my courtroom under better circumstances, Mr. Momet."

A few snickers sounded in the courtroom.

Momet grinned. "Yes, sir."

Many would remember the last time he'd been in the courtroom two years ago when he was tried and found guilty for killing his girlfriend in 1891. He'd served several months at the prison in Marquette before Myrtle uncovered the truth: that Mr. Pfrommer had committed the crime.

Today he was testifying as owner of the local hardware store.

"Mr. Momet," said Jake, holding up the coil of clothesline, "are you familiar with this type of clothesline?"

"Yah. Dat's da only kind we sell at da store."

"Do you recall Mr. Thatcher purchasing clothesline like this?"

"Yah. Last fall. He said his son was movin' in wit him and dey was goin' to be doin' more laundry. He needed new clothesline."

"And do you ever recall selling clothesline like this to Professor Thatcher?"

"Nah. I never even met da professor. He never come into my store, not that I know of, anyways."

Jake walked back to his desk and sat down.

"Mr. Draper?" said Judge Hurstbourne.

"Mr. Momet, are you the only store in town that sells clothesline?"

"Far as I know, yah."

"How about other towns around?"

"Huh?"

"Are there stores in other towns that sell this brand of clothesline?"

"Maybe—I don't know," said Momet.

"Thank you," said Draper. "No more questions."

Judge Hurstbourne glanced up at the clock: a few minutes past eleven—too early to adjourn for lunch.

"Mr. Draper, are you ready to call your first witness?" he asked.

"I am, Your Honor. The defense calls Mrs. Tallulah Redman to the stand."

Sporting a full-length skirt, Tallulah swished her way to the witness box, a big smile on her face. Her red hair spilled out in curls, almost covering the dangling earrings she was wearing. It was obvious she was enjoying her moment in the spotlight.

"...I do," she said, taking her oath.

"Mrs. Redman, you were a close friend of Edwin Thatcher, the deceased, were you not?" asked Draper.

"Close? We was engaged to be married—until he all of a sudden ups and breaks it off."

"How long had you known the Professor?"

"I met him right after my Banji died—'bout seven years ago."

"And who was Banji?"

"My husband—rest his soul." Tallulah made the sign of the cross on her breast.

"Why did Professor Thatcher end your engagement?" asked Draper.

"Hell if I know! Just up and done it—no explanation, nothin'."

"I understand he also wrote you out of his will."

"Objection!" shouted Jake, scrambling to his feet. "I see where Mr. Draper's going with this. Mrs. Redman is not on trial."

"You're right;" said Judge Hurstbourne, "sustained."

"Mrs. Redman, you say you found the note in the pocket

of the professor's coat—the one addressed to Miss Tully."

"It weren't no note, it was a envelope. And, yah, I found it in da coat."

"Yes, an envelope," said Draper. "Mrs. Redman, how do we know you didn't write that note yourself to throw suspicion on Mr. Thatcher?"

"Objection, Your Honor!" Jake cried again. "No basis in fact, and he's *still* trying to implicate the witness in the murder."

"Sustained," said Judge Hurstbourne. "Mr. Draper, you are warned: Mrs. Redman is not on trial here. Pursue another line of questioning."

"I have no more questions, Your Honor," said Draper.

"Cross examine, Jake?" asked the judge.

"Yes, thank you, Judge. Mrs. Redman, do you know if Professor Thatcher owned the type of clothesline that has been placed into evidence?"

"Not hardly. He didn't have no clothesline at all; didn't need none."

"Why is that?"

"'Cause I did all his laundry—for the last five years. I don't know who did it 'fore that."

"So he had no poles in his yard for a clothesline?"

"Oh, da poles were dere, all right; just din't have no line on dem."

"What kind of clothesline do you have, Mrs. Redman?" asked Jake.

"Wire."

"Mrs. Redman, did you have anything to do with the murder of Edwin Thatcher?"

"No!" Tallulah cried out. "I loved dat old bastard. I'da never hurt him."

"Thank you, Mrs. Redman."

"Mr. Draper?" said Judge Hurstbourne.

"The defense calls Mrs. Alice Jones."

"Mrs. Jones," said Draper, once Alice was sworn in, "you live next door to Mr. Thatcher and his son; is that right?"

"Yah."

"And on the day of Professor Thatcher's murder, did you see Mr. Thatcher and his son leave?"

"Yah, I did."

"What time was that?"

"I'd say about tree or four—somewhere in dere."

"And did you see them return?" asked Draper.

"Nah, not dat day. Dey din't come back 'til da next day."

"Was it usual for either of them to be gone overnight?"

"Nah," said Alice. "Dey was always home and in bed by nine o'clock."

"In bed?"

Alice blushed. "I *guess* dey was in bed; da lights were always off by den."

"Did Mr. Thatcher happen to mention where they were going?"

"Nah."

"The next day did he tell you where they had been?"

"Nah. Dey just showed up."

"And what time was that?" asked Draper.

"'Bout 'leven, I reckon."

"Now, the constable stopped by later on the day Mr. Thatcher and his son left; is that correct?"

"Yah, him and dat nice Miss Tully."

Alice glanced at Myrtle and smiled.

"Besides them, did you see anyone else at the Thatcher home that day?" asked Draper.

"Yah, earlier dat day, 'bout an hour after Mr. Thatcher and his son left, some stranger showed up—a man."

"You'd never seen this man before?"

"Nah, never seed him before."

"Can you describe the man?"

"Not really. He had on a long fur coat. Oh, and a chook on his head. He had a big scarf wrapped around da bottom of his face. I tink he might have been wearin' glasses."

"And what did the man do?"

"First, he knocked on da door," said Alice. "Den he went 'round back."

"And what did he do back there?" asked Draper.

Alice shrugged. "I don't know; I couldn't see him. Din't see him no more once he went 'round back."

"Could you have seen if the man entered the shed?"

Alice looked at Draper, slow to understand.

"Nah, 'cause like I said, he was in da back. I was still in my livin' room."

"So he *could* have entered the shed or even the house?" asked Draper.

"Objection," said Jake. "Calls for speculation."

"Sustained," said Judge Hurstbourne.

"Thank you, Mrs. Jones. No further questions."

Judge Hurstbourne looked at Jake. "Mr. McIntyre?"

"Mrs. Jones," said Jake, "did Mr. Thatcher or Lincoln ever tell you how they felt about Professor Thatcher?"

"Objection, Your Honor," said Draper. "Calls for hearsay."

"Sustained," said the judge.

"No further questions," said Jake.

"Mr. Draper," said Judge Hurstbourne, "your next witness?"

"I call Mrs. Rebecca Darling to the stand, Your Honor."

CHAPTER TWENTY-FIVE

Seventy-two-years old, Eunice Rebecca Darling had been born in Booker Falls before it even *was* Booker Falls. She had lived there her whole life. Her husband had died when she was only thirty-five. By then he had become a wealthy man and had left her a generous estate that she used to purchase the farmhouse that she converted into a boarding house.

There was little that had gone on in the town in her seven decades of life she didn't know about.

For her day in the limelight, she had decided to apply a touch of makeup and lipstick, though nothing like Tallulah had worn. She also had on her best Sunday dress and the earrings she'd received on her last birthday, dangly ones, each sporting two turquoise globes, one half-way down the gold chains, the other hanging loose at the bottom.

"Doesn't she look pretty?" whispered Daisy.

Myrtle nodded.

"Mrs. Darling," said Draper, "you were familiar with both of the Thatchers—Orville and Edwin?"

"I was."

"You were also familiar with Caroline Thatcher?"

"Oh, yah, I knew Caroline."

"What can you tell us about her marriage to Mr. Thatcher?"

"Objection," said Jake. He didn't bother to stand up this time. "Hearsay."

"I'll allow it," said Judge Hurstbourne.

"What?" cried Jake, jumping to his feet—jumping being a relative term for how fast Jake could move. "Your Honor, when I asked Mrs. Jones if Mr. Thatcher or Lincoln ever told her how they felt about Professor Thatcher you upheld Mr. Draper's objection."

"Now, Mr. Mcintyre," said the judge, "this ain't the same, is it? You were asking what a third party said; Mr. Draper has asked Mrs. Darling about her own observations. The motion is denied. You may take your seat, Mr. McIntyre."

Scowling, Jake sat back down.

"Now, Mrs. Darling, your observation, please," said Draper.

"Well, sir, it was somewhat of a scandal, I can tell you dat," said Mrs. Darling. "Edwin, he'd went off to college, somewhere downstate I tink. Everybody knew him and Caroline were sweet on each other. I'd heard dey was plannin' on gettin' married when Edwin finished school. I don't know how it happened but somehow Caroline and Orville, dey got involved and 'fore you knowed it dey up and run off and got hitched. I know Caroline's parents tought it was scandalous and I'm pretty sure Mr. and Mrs. Thatcher weren't none too happy, neither."

"Objection," said Jake. "Calls for speculation."

"I'll give you this one, Mr. McIntyre," said Judge Hurstbourne. "The jury will disregard Mrs. Darling's last statement about the Thatchers."

"Go on, Mrs. Darling," said Draper.

"When Edwin got back home and found out what happened, boy was he mad."

"Objection," said Jake, "calls for facts not in evidence."

"Let me rephrase," said Draper. "Did you see anything that indicated to you that Edwin was upset with his brother?"

"First off, I knowed it when he whacked Orville in da head wit a two by four."

"Edwin attacked Orville?"

"Yah, right out dere on Main Street. I was comin' out o' da dry goods store and I saw Edwin chasin' Orville down da street. When he caught up to him he whacked him a good one."

"Anything else?"

"Oh, yah. Richie found out—"

"Richie?"

"Richie Barnoble—he'd just been made constable. He found out and he went and arrested Edwin and trew him in jail. His daddy wouldn't bail him out. Edwin and me was friends, so I asked my husband if he wouldn't bail him out. I went down to da jail wit him and when Edwin got out he was still mad. He told me he wished he'd killed Orville."

Mrs. Darling shook her head in a disapproving manner. "Dey was never close after dat."

"And then, there was the accident five years ago," said Draper.

"Yah, dat was horrible. Poor Caroline was killed. Orville admitted he was drunk and he was drivin' da carriage too fast. It din't make it 'round da curve and Caroline was trown out. 'Cordin' to da doc, she died instantly. I saw Edwin at her funeral. He told me again den he was sorry he hadn't killed Orville years earlier."

"And how did Orville feel toward his brother?"

"I don't suppose an objection would do any good?" asked Jake.

The judge shook his head.

"I tink Orville was sorry for everting dat had happened," said Mrs. Darling.

"How about the cabin?" asked Draper.

"Oh, yah, he was upset 'bout dat, sure 'nough. Said it made it so he couldn't never fish no more."

"Was he upset enough to kill Professor Thatcher?"

"Objection," said Jake, "calls for speculation."

"Sustained," said Judge Hurstbourne.

"Your witness," said Draper, turning to Jake.

Jake hesitated for a moment. He would have liked to have known Mrs. Darling's answer to the question he'd just objected to, but he was afraid it might not be what he wanted to hear.

"No questions," he said.

"Do you have any more witnesses?" Judge Hurstbourne asked Draper.

"Yes, sir, I will be calling two more: Orville Thatcher and Lincoln Thatcher."

"Ooh," whispered Myrtle, "so he *is* going to have them testify. Mr. McIntyre says it's always a bad move for the accused when they testify."

"I guess we'll have to see," whispered Daisy.

"Okay." said the judge. "Accordin' to that big clock on the wall it's lunchtime, so I reckon we'll pick this up later. Court adjourned 'til one-thirty. We'll hear your first witness at that time, Mr. Draper."

*****

"Want to get a bite at Miss Madeline's?" asked Daisy.

"Sure. I hear they're serving tomato bisque today," said Myrtle.

"While that sounds delicious, I'm going to have the meatloaf and mashed potatoes."

"I don't understand how you stay so slim and trim with all you eat."

Daisy's eyebrows raised. "Have you *looked* at me lately?"

"I bet Eddie has no complaints," said Myrtle.

"No, he seems perfectly content with me just the way I am," said Daisy, a big grin stretched across her face.

*****

Although Miss Madeline's was packed with everyone who had been attending the trial, Myrtle and Daisy managed to find a table by the front window. As soon as they were seated and ordered lunch Daisy was off to the ladies' room.

Myrtle stared at the courthouse across the street. She still considered it the ugliest building she had ever seen.

Gray, built of concrete, it paled in comparison to all the other buildings on the street which were painted in various bright colors, meant to produce at least a modicum of pleasure—an attempt to lift the spirits of those who had to endure the harsh winters of Michigan's Upper Peninsula.

And the building's interior was no better than the exterior.

Dark brown walls with nothing to break their starkness: no photographs, no paintings, no mirrors, no murals—nothing. The handrails, an even darker shade than the walls, dulled from the accumulated grime of countless hands over the years, were concave in shape and so large in diameter that a normal woman's hand couldn't fit around it.

Built in 1880 to replace the original courthouse that had stood for forty-six years before it burned to the ground—a case of arson attributed to the losing party in a particularly rancorous lawsuit—the whole building, inside and out, exuded a somber aura, a sense that this was a place where serious matters were decided.

The one redeeming quality the courthouse possessed was that it also held the offices of both Henri and George.

Henri and George—Henri *or* George. *That* was the quandary Myrtle was faced with. Both wanted to marry her. She knew she had to make a decision.

But not right now. Daisy had rejoined her and was already wolfing down her meatloaf.

Myrtle stirred her soup.

Sometime, she thought. But not today.

CHAPTER TWENTY-SIX

Orville Thatcher had already been sworn in by the time Myrtle and Daisy returned to the courtroom.

"Mr. Thatcher," said Draper, "please give the jury an account of your time on the day your brother was murdered, beginning with when you received the note he sent to you."

"Objection, Your Honor," said Jake. "Calls for facts not in evidence—it has not been established there was a note, let alone that it was sent by Professor Thatcher."

"Sustained."

"Then let's establish it," said Draper. "Mr. Thatcher, on the day your brother was killed, did you receive a note from him asking you to meet him at a cabin on the Portage River?"

"Yah, I did;" said Orville, "about tree in da afternoon. I looked out da window and I saw dis feller coming up to da door. When I opened it, he handed me an envelope. I tanked him, and he spun around and moseyed off."

"Was the envelope addressed to you?" asked Draper.

"Nah, sir, it din't have no writin' on it at all."

"What was in the envelope?" asked Draper.

"I closed da door 'cause it was cold, ya know. I went in

and opened da envelope and it was a note from Edwin. He wanted to meet me out at da cabin."

"Did the note say why he wanted to meet with you?"

"Nah, just said it was important. I figured he wanted me to get my stuff out of da cabin 'cause he was goin' to sell it."

"Why didn't you call him to find out why he wanted to meet you?" asked Draper.

"I don't have no phone. Ain't had one for years, now."

"What did you do then?"

"I don't have no carriage no more, neither; and no sleigh. Had to sell both of dem after I had to stop fishing. I asked Lincoln if'n he couldn't borrow Mr. Middleton's car or sometin' and drive me over dere. He's out of town now, ya know, down in Floreeda and Lincoln is looking after his place. So, Lincoln did, he brought da sleigh, and we headed over for da cabin. Edwin wasn't dere, so we waited for him. But he never showed up. By den it was too dark to come back home so we spent da night in da cabin and come back da next day."

"And what happened the next day after you arrived back home?"

"Lincoln, he took da sleigh back to Mr. Middleton's. I tought 'bout walkin' over to Edwin's place to see why he din't show up, but den I figured if'n he wanted to see me, let him come to my place."

"Then what happened?"

"That afternoon da constable and dat nice Miss Tully came by and told me Edwin had been killed. Den Lincoln come in. We all chatted for a while and den da constable and Miss Tully, dey left."

"And when was the next time the constable came to your home?" asked Draper.

"A couple weeks ago when he come to arrest me and

Lincoln."

"He really came to search your place, didn't he, with a warrant?"

"Yah, but den he arrested us."

"What did the constable show you he found at your residence and in your shed?"

"Da knife and some insurance policy."

"And clothesline?" asked Draper. "And a marlinspike?"

"Well, yah, but dat stuff was mine."

"And the other items?"

"Dey ain't mine. I never seed dat knife before and I don't know nothin' 'bout dat dere insurance policy."

"But the constable says you admitted it was your signature on the application," said Draper.

"Yah, I said dat. But after tinkin' it over, I ain't so sure dat's my signature."

"You mean someone forged your signature?"

"Yah;" said Orville, "dat's what I'm tinkin'."

"And you have no idea how either the knife or the policy came to be in your possession?"

"Dey weren't in my possession—dey was in my house and my shed."

"Do you keep your house and shed locked?"

"Locked? What for? Ain't nothin' in either of dem worth stealin'."

"One last question, Mr. Thatcher. Did you kill your brother, Edwin Thatcher?"

"Heck, no! We sure didn't see eye to eye but I din't kill him."

"No more questions, Your Honor."

"Mr. McIntyre?" said the judge.

Jake stood and walked over to the jury box. He put one hand on it, bracing himself.

"Mr. Thatcher," he said, "what happened to the note you say you got from your brother?"

"I troo it in da fire at da cabin."

Jake turned toward Thatcher.

"So, there's no way to substantiate if you're telling us the truth, that you even got a note."

"If'n my word ain't good enough for you, den I guess not," said Orville.

"Was the note handwritten or typed?" asked Jake, walking over to Thatcher.

"Typed—why?"

"Did your brother sign his name on it?"

"No. It was all typed."

"How do you know it was from your brother, then?" asked Jake.

"Who else would want to meet me at da cabin?" asked Orville. "Dat's a stupid question."

"Is there anyone who can confirm you and your son spent the night in the cabin the evening Edwin Thatcher was killed?"

Orville shook his head. "Nah, don't reckon dere is."

"Mrs. Darling testified she heard you threaten to kill your brother. Do you recollect saying that?"

"If Mrs. Darling says I did, den I did 'cause I know she's no liar. But dat was fifty years ago. If'n I wanted to kill him don't you tink I would of done it 'fore now?"

"No more questions," said Jake.

"Your Honor, I call Lincoln Thatcher to the stand," said Draper.

"Mr. Thatcher," said Draper once Lincoln was sworn in, "you heard the testimony your father gave. Do you agree with the sequence of events as he described them? Do you have anything more to add?"

"Only that I was fond of Uncle Edwin," said Lincoln. "I would never hurt him. I know him and my dad, dey didn't get along but him and me, we were friends. And why would I kill him just to get my inheritance sooner? Joker said he'd wait for da money. It don't make sense."

"Did you see the note your father said he received from your uncle?"

"Yah, he showed it to me."

"Did you see whoever it was who delivered it?"

"Nah, I didn't see him."

"Lincoln, did you kill your uncle, Edwin Thatcher?"

"No, sir, I sure did not."

"No more questions, Your Honor."

"I hear my dinner calling," said Judge Hurstbourne. "Seein' as how tomorrow is Good Friday there'll be no court. Mr. McIntyre, if you can wait 'til Monday to question Mr. Thatcher . . .?"

The judge stared at Jake, waiting for an answer.

"Oh…yes, Your Honor, that will be fine," said Jake.

"Then," said the judge, "we shall adjourn until ten o'clock Monday morning. Mr. Draper, Mr. McIntyre, that should also provide each of you ample time to prepare your closing statements."

CHAPTER TWENTY-SEVEN

"I wish you and Eddie were going with us tomorrow," said Myrtle.

She and Daisy had persuaded Mrs. Darling to let them take their dessert from dinner—peach cobbler—into the parlor. Henri and Pierre were involved in an arcane discussion of Fournier d'Albe's 1907 book, *Two New Worlds*, with Pierre leaning toward d'Albe's view of an unseen spiritual universe and Henri insisting that one universe—the one in which we lived—was, by definition of the word, the only one.

"Otherwise," said Henri, "why do they call it a *uni*verse?"

"Yeah, me too," said Daisy as she retrieved a large portion of the cobbler with her fork. "But he's gotta work. Being the fire chief's not all it's cracked up to be. So, what are you two going to do over in Red Jacket?"

"First we're going to go skating at the Colosseum, then have lunch at the Michigan House. I might even get him to let me do a little shopping at Vertin's."

"The Michigan House," said Daisy. "Now I really do wish I was going. I haven't been there since you and I went last year."

"Where I found Herman Hutchinson's coat—"

"—which proved that that poor Lars Jørgensen didn't kill your boss."

"I don't suppose anything like that will happen on this trip," said Myrtle.

Daisy looked at her and smiled. "I wouldn't bet on it, knowing you."

*****

Myrtle leaned back in her seat and closed her eyes. She always enjoyed it when someone else drove. The drive she had made from New Orleans to Booker Falls two and a half years earlier had cured her of any more long trips by herself.

Besides, she liked Henri's car. It was considerably more comfortable than her rickety old 1907 Model N.

Maybe it's time I got a new car, Myrtle thought. *Okay, a newer* car.

There was still snow on the ground, but between the trees, fields with patches of green peeked through. Spring came late in the Keweenaw, but come it eventually did, and summer always followed. Myrtle appreciated the change of seasons here more than in Louisiana, where the differences weren't as extreme.

"You asleep?"

Henri's voice caused her to open her eyes. She looked at him.

"I don't think so. Why—was I snoring?"

"No, you've just been unusually quiet. Not like you at all."

"Ha!" said Myrtle. "You just *think* I talk a lot. You should have met my mother. She would talk even while she played her violin—which was no easy feat considering she had it tucked under her chin."

"I'm looking forward to lunch," said Henri.

"I'm looking forward to the skating;" Myrtle countered,

"especially at the Colosseum. Is it as grand as it's made out to be?"

"Grander. The place is only eight years old. And you won't believe how big it is."

Myrtle leaned back and closed her eyes again. The steady huummm of the tires on the road produced a feeling of relaxation. The *whoosh* of trees rushing by on either side added to her sense of contentment.

She loved the life she now had; it was comfortable, safe, satisfying. She wondered that in such a short time this little town of Booker Falls nestled in the backwoods of Michigan's Upper Peninsula had become such a part of her—this little corner of the world she now called home. But it was more than that—it was her life, her *place* in life, where she belonged. She couldn't imagine being anywhere else. And she loved her job as head librarian at the college library.

Still, she wondered if it was what she was cut out for for the rest of her life.

She had helped solve no less than five murders since she had arrived here, a feat that had left her with a sense of . . . of what? Accomplishment? Fulfillment?

Searching for clues, putting two and two together and coming out with more than four—it was exhilarating. Even having her life threatened by the suspects had been both frightening and exciting.

Three years ago, after she came back to America from France, she had wondered what was next for her. It hadn't been a bad life up to then. She had a loving family: a mother who was a professional musician, a violinist with New Orleans' first city orchestra, and a father, a kind and gentle man, who was active in local politics but who never missed dinner at home with his wife and daughter.

She regretted she had no siblings, nor an abundance of

close friends growing up.

While she would have preferred to have attended public school, her parents insisted on enrolling her at The Academy of the Sacred Heart, a Catholic school for girls, a decision to which Myrtle had always attributed her uneasiness around boys and, later, men.

She still to this day wasn't sure why, after graduating high school, she had entered Ursuline Convent. That lasted less than a year. She'd left the convent and got a telephone operator's job at the local office of American Telephone and Telegraph. Six years later when General John Pershing, Commander of the Allied Expeditionary Force in Europe, deciding he could no longer abide the unreliable French telephone system, had set up his own and recruited some four hundred and fifty women who were fluent in both English and French—which Myrtle was—to serve as operators, she had jumped at the chance.

She smiled, remembering the uniform she'd been issued: a dark blue wool Norfolk jacket with a long matching skirt; a white blouse; black, high-top shoes and brown army boots; a hat, an overcoat, a rubber raincoat, and woolen underwear. And the black sateen bloomers she'd had to wear under her skirt!

It had been a life-expanding experience. Then, two years later, when the war ended and she was on her way home, she'd stopped in Paris.

That was when she met Thomas.

She smiled at the memory.

She and three of the girls she worked with had gone to a cabaret, the Le Chat Noir on Boulevard de Clichy, where they spent the evening drinking cheap wine and listening to musicians and poets. They'd been joined by three men, two of them French and the third an Englishman who had come to Paris before the war to study at the École des Beaux-Arts—or so Myrtle thought at the time.

She had ended up at the Englishman's—Thomas's—apartment. She even remembered the number: eleven, Boulevard de Clichy, the former residence of Pablo Picasso.

They'd spent the night together and made love—twice.

The next morning she took a taxi back to the boarding house where she was staying, sure she would never see Thomas again.

Then, eighteen months ago, he showed up at the library.

She remembered how she'd felt when he walked—

"Are you having a good dream?"

Myrtle opened her eyes and blinked, then looked at Henri, seated next to her in the car.

"What?" she said.

"A good dream? You were grinning, then smiling. It looked like you were having a good dream."

"I wasn't asleep."

"Oh, okay, I thought you were."

"No," said Myrtle, embarrassed she'd been thinking of Thomas. "I was just . . . just reminiscing."

"About the good old days?" asked Henri, chuckling.

"Yeah, the good old days," Myrtle answered. "Are we getting close?"

"Twenty minutes to Houghton, then on to Red Jacket."

Myrtle leaned back and closed her eyes again.

*****

"Myrtle, wake up. We're here."

Myrtle opened her eyes and blinked.

I guess I really was asleep this time, she thought.

She sat up straighter in her seat and gazed at the huge structure looming before her. Three stories high with a barrel roof, it reminded her of the Bessonneau tents she had seen in

France, hangars for airplanes, except this was considerably larger.

"Wow, that is big," she said.

"Wait 'til you see the inside," said Henri.

Henri was right. Myrtle was even more impressed by the interior of the colosseum.

"Quick," said Myrtle, "let's get our skates on. I can't wait to get out on the ice."

*****

They'd been skating for a little more than an hour. Myrtle was surprised to discover how skilled Henri was.

"You grew up in the Caribbean," she said. "How'd you learn to skate like that?"

"Ah, yes," said Henri as he completed a camel spin, "but I went to college in Booker Falls. You had to learn to skate to play hockey—and, of course, *everybody* played hockey. I had a good teacher."

"Who was that?" asked Myrtle, coming off a bracket turn.

"George. You know, he played hockey in college. That's how he hurt his leg."

"Oh, yes, I'd forgotten. He doesn't skate any more, does he?"

"Not much," said Henri. "A shame, too. He was really good. How about some hot chocolate?"

"Oooh, that sounds delicious!"

While they sat and drank their hot chocolates, Henri told Myrtle about the first time he had been in the colosseum.

"It was seven years ago," he said. "I was teaching school at the time. George heard there was going to be a new car show here in Red Jacket. He wanted me to come with him. I didn't want to—I thought they were merely a passing fancy."

"Until I showed up in town driving one," said Myrtle, grinning.

Henri smiled. "Yah, well at first. I still didn't care for them, especially seein' as how you almost ran me and Jessie down."

Myrtle chuckled. "That *was* a close call, wasn't it?"

"Anyway," Henri continued, "George and I drove over here. There must have been a couple dozen cars in here, lined up around the sides and down the middle."

"On the ice?" asked Myrtle.

"No, no ice. George and I spent about two hours walking around. He thought about getting one but decided not to."

"Again, until I came along," said Myrtle.

"Yah, you were the ruination of the town," said Henri, laughing.

"That was before what happened to Lydia, wasn't it?"

Henri's face hardened. Lydia's death was not something he liked to think about.

"Yah, the year before."

"I'm sorry," said Myrtle, taking his hand. "I didn't mean to dredge up an unpleasant memory."

Henri's face softened. "Nah, it's okay. It was a long time ago."

"You really loved her, didn't you?"

Henri looked away but not before Myrtle saw a single tear escape his eye.

"Yah, I did." He turned back and faced Myrtle. "But now I love you."

Neither of them spoke for a moment.

Finally, Henri said, "Let's skate some more and then go get a bite to eat."

A feeling of relief came over Myrtle. "Sounds good to me," she said, getting to her feet. "Race you to the end of the building," she yelled, taking off.

"No fair!" shouted Henri, scurrying off after her.

*****

Entering the Michigan House, Myrtle felt a sense of familiarity. She had only been here three times since she'd moved to Booker Falls, twice with Daisy and once with George following an enjoyable afternoon at the Calumet Theatre. But it just felt right, a place where she was comfortable.

Plus, she remembered, the food had always been almost beyond scrumptious.

Though it was April and the weather had begun to improve—it was thirty-seven when they left the boarding house that morning—the roaring fire in the fireplace was a welcome sight.

As the two of them followed the waitress to their table, Myrtle glanced up at the large ceiling mural that stretched above the enormous wooden bar, a rendering of a picnic, where brew readily flowed. It was one of the things she loved about the place.

*****

"My, that was delicious," said Myrtle. She dabbed her lips with her napkin. "I worked up an appetite with all that skating."

"Did you enjoy the prime rib?" asked Henri.

"I guess I'm a red meat kind of gal," said Myrtle, smiling. "The other times I've eaten here I had the beef tenderloin and the beef and kidney bean chili. Oh, but one time I strayed—I had the Wild Mushroom Ravioli." A pensive look came over her. "Now that I think of it, I believe it was my favorite. I may have it again the next time I'm here."

Henri laid down his napkin and looked into Myrtle's eyes.

"I need to know," he said, "if you have decided to accept my proposal. It's been two months since I asked you to marry me. I'd like an answer."

Myrtle inhaled and wadded her napkin up in her clenched fists.

She didn't speak for a few minutes. Then . . . "Henri, I just don't know. I don't know if I'm ready to get married."

"Is it that?" asked Henri. "Or is it George?"

"George?"

"I've heard he's also asked you to marry him. Are you considering his offer?"

Myrtle stared at her now empty plate. "It's not that. I . . . I just don't know."

They were both startled by the waiter who suddenly appeared from nowhere.

"Are you ready for dessert?" he asked.

"No, thanks, not for me," said Myrtle, looking up.

"Me, neither," said Henri. "We're ready for our check."

Henri watched the waiter walk away, then turned to Myrtle.

"I won't bother asking again," he said.

*****

True to form, Daisy was waiting in the parlor when Henri and Myrtle walked through the front door. She watched as Henri silently climbed the stairs. Myrtle came in and sat down across from her.

"I'm no expert but I'm guessing you didn't have all that good a time," said Daisy.

Myrtle sighed. "It was fine 'til dinner. I loved the ice skating—the colosseum is fabulous. Dinner later at the Michigan House was exquisite."

Daisy raised her arms in a gesture that indicated 'so what went wrong?'

"He asked me if I had made up my mind."

"About marrying him?"

Myrtle nodded.

"And what did you say?" asked Daisy.

Myrtle shrugged. "I said I didn't know."

Daisy shook her head. "Girl, you better make up your mind. Neither one of those men is going to wait forever."

CHAPTER TWENTY-EIGHT

Myrtle was glad when the weekend was over.

Saturday hadn't been too bad; she had worked her regular day at the library. When she arrived back at the boarding house that evening, there was no one around. She found out later Daisy was out with Eddie.

Sunday morning after breakfast—notable by Henri's absence—she and Mrs. Darling had walked to church. It was a beautiful Easter service. Afterward Mrs. Darling prepared a special Easter meal. Again, Henri was nowhere to be seen.

Daisy had invited Eddie over to join her, Myrtle, Pierre, and Mrs. Darling to view a set of slides on the Holy Land in the Magic Lantern the latter had received a few days earlier from Sears & Roebuck. Mrs. Darling had made her traditional Easter punch—strawberry and orange gelatin for the base with pineapple juice and ginger ale—as well as her famous Easter egg sugar cookies.

Daisy had warned Pierre and Eddie not to ask about Henri's absence. Still, Myrtle felt as though a shroud hung over everything and she was pretty sure it was her fault.

*****

At ten o'clock on Monday morning, she and Daisy settled into their seats at the courthouse for what was to be the final day of the trial.

"Mr. McIntyre," said Judge Hurstbourne, "are you ready to question the witness?"

"I am, Your Honor."

Jake rose to his feet and approached Lincoln.

"Mr. Thatcher, Mr. Mulhearn testified that you received your black eye by falling into a door. Is that true? And I might remind you that perjury—telling a lie while under oath—is punishable by law carrying a penalty of up to fifteen years in prison."

Lincoln hesitated for a minute before answering.

"Nah, dat ain't true."

"And how did you come to receive your black eye?"

"Joker punched me."

"He punched you?"

"Yah, he punched me. In da eye."

"Because you owed him money?"

"Yah, because I owed him money."

"But you had an agreement with Mr. Mulhearn, did you not, that he would give you extra time to pay your debt to him?"

"Well…" Lincoln hesitated. "Not right den I din't, no."

"No? When did you make the agreement with Mr. Mulhearn?"

"Right after he punched me in da eye."

The room erupted in laughter.

"Order, order," shouted Judge Hurstbourne, rapping his gavel on the desk.

"And how long was Mr. Mulhearn going to give you to pay off your debt?"

"Until Uncle Edwin died," answered Lincoln.

"It was open-ended then?" asked Jake.

"Huh?"

"There was no set time limit on how long he would wait?"

"You mean Joker?"

"Yes, Mr. Mulhearn. Did he set any other time limit besides when your uncle died?"

"I guess he did mention someting like dat."

"Something like that...how long?"

"Tree months. He said he'd give me tree months...unless Uncle Edwin died 'fore then."

"And what would have happened if Professor Thatcher was still alive at the end of that time? What would Joker have done to you?"

Lincoln's face paled. "I reckon he probably would have killed me."

"Killed you?"

"Yah...I reckon."

"Instead of taking a chance that your uncle might not die within three months and that Mr. Mulhearn would seek you out and kill you, you decided to take the sure path: to go ahead and kill your uncle right away and get your inheritance so you could pay off Mr. Mulhearn. Is that right?"

At the same time that Draper leaped to his feet ready to object, Lincoln jumped up from the witness chair. "Nah, dat ain't right at all!" he shouted. "I din't kill my uncle. I'da never done dat!"

"I withdraw the question," said Jake, retreating to the safety of his desk. "No further questions, Your Honor."

"Mr. Thatcher, you are excused," said Judge Hurstbourne.

"Mr. Draper," said Judge Hurstbourne, "are you ready for your closing statement?"

"Your Honor, might we have a five minute recess?" asked Draper.

"Five minute recess," said the judge.

"Wow," whispered Daisy, "do you think what Mr. McIntyre did there might have any effect on the jury?"

"It sure couldn't have hurt;" said Myrtle, "although it was only a hypothesis."

Five minutes later the bailiff called the trial back to order.

"Ready now, Mr. Draper?" asked the judge.

"I am, Your Honor," said Draper.

He rose and walked over to the jury box.

"Ladies and gentlemen," he began, "it would seem the prosecution has laid out a very persuasive case against my clients. So persuasive, I feel, that I don't see how you could possibly bring any verdict other than guilty."

A murmur went through the spectators.

"What's he trying to do?" whispered Daisy.

Myrtle shook her head.

"And therein lies the problem," Draper continued. "Their case is *too* perfect. They have provided motives for each of my clients: for Orville Thatcher that he stood to receive an insurance payout of ten thousand dollars; for Lincoln, that he would inherit the deceased's estate and, as we heard before the recess, the wild accusation that Lincoln couldn't wait. The problem with each of those motives, however, is that, first of all, Orville claims he had no knowledge of the insurance policy, that he did not purchase it despite the fact it appears—and I emphasize that word, *appears*—that it is his signature on the application.

"In Lincoln's case, while he was aware he was the sole beneficiary to Professor Thatcher's estate, he knew the professor was dying of cancer, that, indeed, death was imminent—the doctor had said so—and all he had to do was wait a short period of time—nowhere close to three months—before he would inherit his uncle's estate.

"Now, as far as alibis are concerned, it is true my clients cannot provide witnesses who can confirm they were at the cabin on the Portage River that night. At the same time, the prosecution has provided no witnesses placing either of my clients at the scene of the crime. Ladies and gentlemen, Orville Thatcher and Lincoln Thatcher are not stupid. They didn't go to college like Professor Thatcher, but they did graduate from high school. If they killed the professor and are making up the alibi they have given, wouldn't they have been smart enough to have someone vouch for them that they were at the cabin? The reason they don't have anyone is because, since they didn't kill Professor Thatcher, they didn't know they would even *need* an alibi."

While Draper addressed the jurors, Myrtle studied each of them to see their reactions. One woman, in particular, caught her eye, as she seemed to be nodding at everything he said.

"Fingerprints—Orville's prints were nowhere to be found," said Draper, "either in the house or the workshop. Lincoln's were there because, as he testified, he often visited his uncle.

"And, as far as the physical evidence is concerned, the first thing you must consider is that so far no murder weapon has been found. The knife discovered in the Thatcher's shed could not have been it, according to Doctor Sherman. Nor can the blood on the knife be undeniably attributed to the deceased. While the clothesline from the shed was the same type used to bind Professor Thatcher, that clothesline is readily available not only in the local hardware store but in numerous stores I have checked throughout this area.

"The note left for Miss Tully, written by Professor Thatcher and indicating his belief that Orville was threatening him harm has to be considered for what it is: unfounded paranoia by a man who was in the last stages of his life."

Draper walked back to his desk and took a drink of water. Then he returned to the jury box.

"Now, let's go back to fingerprints, or lack thereof. In addition to the fact that no fingerprints belonging to Orville were found at the scene, there were no fingerprints on the knife, on the insurance application, or on the policy itself. Mr. McIntyre would tell you that my clients wiped off any prints from the knife. Yes, they would have—if either of them were guilty. But so would the real killer or killers who might have placed the knife there. And the application and the policy—and even the envelope they were in—how can they explain that the only prints found on those items were those of Mr. Karhul, the insurance agent who issued the policy?

"Folks, if you don't believe every rejection of the prosecution's case I've just laid out for you, please consider this: as I said, Orville Thatcher and Lincoln Thatcher are not stupid. If they did kill the professor would they be dumb enough to leave the knife and the clothesline in their shed? Would they be dumb enough not to come up with an alibi for which they had witnesses? Would Orville be dumb enough to leave the will just lying around? Would Lincoln be dumb enough not to wait a little bit for his uncle to die a natural death to get his money? I don't think so.

"But here's what I do think. Constable de la Cruz testified he had several other suspects in this case before he settled on Mr. Thatcher and his son, none of whom had alibis any better than my client's, and, who, like my clients, had motives for disposing of Professor Thatcher. He also admitted there were several other possible—and I emphasize that word, *possible* —murder weapons he had come across.

"Now, I am not accusing any of those individuals of this crime; at the same time, I don't believe enough effort has been made to ensure neither they nor anyone else were not involved. I believe whoever killed Professor Thatcher framed Orville and Lincoln Thatcher to make it appear as though they were the perpetrators. I believe the real killer, for some reason, disposed of the murder weapon but left the knife in the shed. I believe the real killer went so far as to forge Orville Thatcher's signature on an insurance application, purchase the policy, and then hid said policy in Mr. Thatcher's desk—though not so well that it could not easily be discovered during a search.

"And who might that have been? By Constable de la Cruz's own admission, no attempt was made to identify the man who showed up at the Thatcher home shortly after they left on the day in question. Mrs. Jones testified the man went around to the rear of the house. She didn't see him back there. He easily had access to both the shed and the house. Mr. Thatcher testified he never kept either of them locked.

"We know it was a man. Could it have been Mr. Murphy? Mr. Vertanen? Carl, Mrs. Redman's brother? He was never even questioned by Constable de la Cruz.

"Ladies and gentlemen, how much reasonable doubt is required to come to the conclusion that, while you may not think my clients innocent of this crime, you also cannot be sure in your minds they are guilty?"

Myrtle looked at the juror who had continued to nod throughout Draper's closing. She had a slight smile on her face and her nodding had increased.

"That being the case, I strongly believe you cannot bring back any other verdict than not guilty. Thank you."

As Draper took his seat, Jake left his desk and approached the jury box.

"I feel I must thank my colleague for making my case against his clients. He was kind enough to point out their motives, the lack of an alibi, the preponderance of evidence—

I'm not sure there's much more I can say…but I shall try.

"Like Mr. Draper, I do not think either Orville or Lincoln is stupid or dumb. What I do think is that they are careless. Criminals make mistakes. Mr. Draper suggested that while the real killer disposed of the murder weapon but left the knife where it could be found, he dismissed the possibility that the marlinspike found in the Thatcher's shed, like the stake, the knitting needle, and the railroad spike he alluded to, could have been the murder weapon.

"And while it is possible the knife might have been placed in the shed by someone other than either of the accused, how far-fetched is the notion that someone would pay good money to purchase an insurance policy on which they would never collect—unless they were the beneficiary—and then, somehow, sneak into the Thatcher home to plant it? That would mean the whole purpose of killing Professor Thatcher may have been to implicate Orville or Lincoln rather than just the act itself.

"I do not think there is any reason, in this case, to consider reasonable doubt because, in truth, what is there to doubt? The accused had both motive and opportunity to commit the crime, no provable alibi, and they failed to adequately cover up their misdeeds afterwards.

"No one else committed this murder. Orville Thatcher and Lincoln Thatcher together killed Professor Edwin Thatcher, they did it for the money, and you must find them guilty as charged. Thank you."

Once Jake was seated, Judge Hurstbourne addressed the jury.

"Members of the jury, you have heard from both the prosecution and the defense. It is now up to you to retire to the jury room and render a decision. Here are some instructions I have for you."

As the judge instructed the jury, Daisy turned to Myrtle.

"So?" she asked.

"If I were a juror," whispered Myrtle, still eyeing the juror who seemed to be in accord with the defense's arguments, "I'm not sure I would be persuaded beyond a reasonable doubt."

"You think they're innocent?" asked Daisy, surprised.

"I didn't say that," answered Myrtle.

"Then I'm not sure what you mean."

"Me neither. Let's get out of here."

*****

Myrtle bounded out of the library and sprinted toward the car where Henri sat, patiently waiting.

"Any word yet?" she asked, settling into the passenger seat.

Henri shook his head. "No, and it's driving Jake crazy. He thought the jury would come back with a guilty verdict in less than an hour."

"Instead, it's been three days," said Myrtle. "Does he think they might find the Thatchers innocent?"

"He says he doesn't see how they can. The evidence is overwhelming."

"Yeah, that's what Mr. Draper said, too. Then he explained how maybe it wasn't."

Henri looked at her. "You don't believe they're innocent, do you?"

Myrtle shrugged. "To tell the truth—I don't know. I mean, you're right—the evidence does seem to be overwhelming."

"And yet?"

"And yet, that's the point. It all seems so neat, so wrapped up in a nice, neat ball."

"That would make sense if they were guilty, wouldn't it?" said Henri.

Myrtle's mouth screwed up. "I guess so."

"Henri," said Mrs. Darling as he and Myrtle came through the door. "That nice Mr. McIntyre called; he wants you to call him back.

Minutes later Henri strode into the kitchen where Myrtle was sitting down to the dinner Mrs. Darling had kept warmed for her. He had a wide grin on his face.

"Well?" asked Myrtle.

"Guilty," said Henri.

"Did Mr. McIntyre say what the holdup was?"

"There was one juror who wasn't convinced beyond a reasonable doubt."

"But she came around."

"Guess so," said Henri, pouring himself a cup of coffee. "What makes you think it was one of the women?"

"Just a guess."

CHAPTER TWENTY-NINE

Myrtle gazed through the window at the bustling room outside her office. It was the end of April and finals were approaching.

She watched as one of the students, a young man she'd seen before once or twice, approached the desk. Lydia had asked if she could leave early, as she had a date that evening. Myrtle said yes so now she was the one staffing the desk.

So young, she thought, eyeing the young man. *Was I ever that young?*

"Hi," she greeted him, when she arrived at the desk.

"Hi," the young man responded. "I'd like to check this book out."

Myrtle glanced at the title: *Language: An Introduction to the Study of Speech.*

"I haven't seen this before," said Myrtle.

"I'm planning on becoming a minister," said the man. "I was told this would be helpful—for giving sermons, you know."

Myrtle nodded, opened the book to the checkout page, and stamped it with a date.

"Is that one of Professor Thatcher's candles?" the man asked.

"Yes, it is," said Myrtle. "Was the professor one of your teachers?"

"No, I only met him once."

Myrtle looked puzzled. "You only met him once? But you're familiar with his candles?"

"He gave me one the time we met. I did a favor for him."

"Oh?"

"I was passing his house a few weeks ago—actually, it was the day he was killed—I guess that's been a month, hasn't it? Anyway, I was walking past on my way to class and he called me over; asked me to run an errand for him. He wanted me to deliver an envelope across town, over in Greytown. I told him sure, I'd be happy to as soon as I got out of class. He said he needed it delivered right away, to make sure I handed it to the guy. Said he'd pay me for doing it immediately. I told him I'd do it for a dollar, but he gave me two dollars. I said that was too much but then he said something really strange."

A thought began to swirl around in Myrtle's mind. She knew to whom the note had been delivered.

"What did he say?" she asked.

"He said, 'well, as Frederick somebody or other said, you can't take it with you.' I asked him where he was going but he didn't say; told me to wait a minute. Then he went in the house and when he came back out he handed me the two dollars and a candle and the envelope. I said thanks and took off. It was clear across town, but I didn't mind—two bucks was two bucks. I guess that evening he was murdered."

"Did you hand the envelope to the person there or just put it in the mailbox?"

"Oh, I handed it to him, just like the professor told me to."

"A young man or an old man?" asked Myrtle.

"Old fellow."

"Did he have a ponytail and a beard?"

"Now that you mention it, he did," said the student. "I thought it kind of odd for an old guy like him—the ponytail. Do you know him?"

"Do you remember the address where you delivered the envelope?" asked Myrtle.

"Sure. It was 233 Donken Street."

"Thanks," said Myrtle. "Yes, I do know him."

*****

Myrtle could hardly wait that evening to tell Henri what she had found out at the library.

"I'm sure that was the note Mr. Thatcher said he received from his brother. It was his address. That would confirm what he said about being asked to meet that evening at the cabin."

"That still doesn't make sense," said Henri. "Why would the professor set up a meeting with Orville when he knew you were coming over. He couldn't be in two places at once."

Myrtle bit her lip, thinking. "I don't know," she said, at last. "But there must have been some good reason. Maybe he forgot he had asked me."

"Until you can come up with it, I don't know there's anything else to be done," said Henri.

CHAPTER THIRTY

George sat in his car, waiting for Myrtle to exit the library. It was Wednesday—one of the nights he was scheduled to pick her up after she got off work. She was taking off early, leaving Lydia to close up.

Paige Turner had telephoned Myrtle the week before to let her know copies of the book she'd had published had arrived and that she was having a book signing this evening at six o'clock. Myrtle had suggested to George that they have dinner at Miss Madeline's and afterward walk on down to the book store.

He agreed. But he also had something else in mind. He was determined this would be the day he would get a definitive answer to his proposal; after all, it had been over two months since he'd first offered his hand in marriage.

In his early thirties, he had never been interested in any woman before Myrtle showed up in Booker Falls. He'd dated a few girls from town during his time in college, but nothing had come of any of them, mostly because they had, without exception, made it clear they had no intention of spending the rest of their lives in some backwater town in the wilderness of

Michigan's Upper Peninsula.

As far as George was concerned, he had no desire to live anywhere else.

After he returned home from college and opened his law practice more than one woman had let it be known she was open to his advances. None interested him enough to see them more than once or twice, usually for dinner at Miss Madeline's.

Myrtle was different. He had never known anyone like her.

He'd been enamored that first day when she motored into town in her old Model N Ford, wearing plaid pants, with curly auburn hair peeking out from under a newsboy's cap. And her voice—like that of someone who might have grown up on a Southern plantation somewhere in Georgia or Mississippi, a soft, lilting sound. New Orleans, he'd found out later.

At the time he couldn't believe how boldly he had acted in stopping by the boarding house the next day and inviting her to the ice cream social. She'd said no. But later on, she'd agreed to other dates.

Over the next two and a half years he'd courted her, painfully aware his best friend, Henri, was also dating her. Finally, he had proposed, only to be put off.

No more. Tonight was the night.

"Hello, George."

He looked up, brought out of his reverie by Myrtle's greeting.

"Hi," he said. "Ready to go? I feel like liver and onions tonight."

"Ooh, that sounds good," said Myrtle, sliding into the passenger's seat.

*****

George parked his touring car under the gas street light

outside the restaurant. Before next winter the town council hoped to replace all of the current lights with electric ones. He hurried around to help Myrtle out of the car but, as usual, she had already stepped down.

Inside they were greeted by the cozy warmth of a blaze in the fireplace and then by Danny, Madeline's grandson.

"Good evening, Mr. Mayor, Miss Tully," he said. "Please sit anywhere you like. I'll be your server tonight."

"Danny, have you been promoted?" asked Myrtle. She had never seen him perform any task at the restaurant other than clearing the tables.

"I have. Grandma says I am now ready to be a server. I know you like Mona, but she's off tonight so I will do my best to fill in."

Myrtle gave him a big smile. "I'm sure you'll do wonderfully."

*****

"I do believe Miss Madeline's serves the best liver and onions in town," said Myrtle, as she wiped her lips with her napkin.

"Considering it's the only place in town that serves liver and onions, I am inclined to agree with you," George replied.

He adjusted the collar on his shirt and leaned back in his chair.

"Myrtle, we need to talk."

"Talk? What about?"

"I asked you to marry me—two months ago. I feel it's time you gave me an answer."

Myrtle nodded. "You're right. It is time. And I have decided to make a commitment."

*****

Myrtle left George behind in the restaurant to pay for the

meal and headed down the street the short distance to Paige Turner's New, Used, and Rare Book Store where she was greeted warmly by both the owner, Paige Turner, and Ginger, the resident cat.

"Myrtle," said Paige, wrapping her arms around her friend, "I haven't seen you since . . . well, I don't know how long it's been. I'm so happy you came tonight."

"Are you kidding? I wouldn't miss this for the world."

Myrtle looked around; the store was packed with customers.

"You have a great turnout for the signing," she said.

"It was Daisy's article in today's paper. She laid it on thick what a big event this was."

"She was right—having a published author in our little town *is* a big event."

"I may have some competition, though," said Paige.

"How so?"

"We got a new book in on Monday: *The Velveteen Rabbit.* It's by a British author, Margery Williams."

"What's it about?"

Paige reached under the counter. When her hand reemerged it held a copy of the book. "It's a children's book about a stuffed rabbit who wants to become real. All the mothers in Greytown are buying a copy for their child—they're telling them it's the Easter bunny that brought their eggs on Sunday."

Myrtle chuckled. "I'd believe it if I were a kid."

"I know they can't really afford the book;" whispered Paige, "so I'm selling them at cost."

"You are a wonderful person, Paige," said Myrtle. "We need more like you."

"I just hope they have enough money left over to buy my book."

Just then a portly woman in her late fifties approached the counter.

"Mrs. Cardiff," said Paige, "you found what you wanted?"

"Yah," said the woman, "dis copy of da *Ladies' Home Journal*. I love dere articles about cooking. My Herbert, he's a big eater when he's home."

"Is he gone a lot?" asked Myrtle.

"Yah, he's a fisherman. Works off da boats over dere on da Portage."

"It was so funny when Mrs. Cardiff found out what my book was about," said Paige.

"I know you told me your book was a children's book. What *is* it about?" asked Myrtle.

"Shoelaces."

"Shoelaces?"

"Yes, you see when I was a child I could never tie my shoes—still can't."

"Everyone knows how to tie shoes," said Myrtle. "Why couldn't you?"

"Because I'm left-handed," said Paige.

"You're left-handed? I never noticed. But what does that have to do with tying your shoelaces?"

"I didn't have anyone to teach me. Both my parents were right-handed. They tried and tried to teach me but they never could. Later on, I discovered that it's nearly impossible for a right-handed person to teach a left-handed person to tie their shoelaces—or a bow. It's all about the direction the lace goes. My book's about a little girl who was left-handed and couldn't tie her laces and how she eventually met a left-handed person who taught her how."

"But you never did?" asked Myrtle. "Learn how to tie your laces?"

Paige shook her head. "Never did. Mrs. Cardiff, tell Myrtle what you told me."

"Yah, like I said, my Herbert, he's a fisherman. So when I was on da jury—"

"Now I recognize you," said Myrtle. "You were on the jury that found Mr. Thatcher and his son guilty."

"Yah, me and Mrs. Oldenmyer. We was surprised dey 'lowed women on da jury. Anyways, I was on da jury but I had a hard time findin' dose two guilty I gotta tell ya. I sorta tought dey was, but I had me doubts. Finally, da rest o' dem, da udder jury members, dey convinced me to vote guilty so's we could go home."

"Why weren't you sure?" asked Myrtle. This was the woman she'd watched nodding her head during Draper's closing argument.

"For sure dere was a lot of evidence dey did it; I mean, da knife and clothesline and dat insurance policy. Dat all made 'em look guilty. But what got me stuck was da bows."

"The bows?" asked Myrtle. "What bows?"

"Da bows—how dat dead man's feet was tied to da chair. You know, in dat photo."

The photograph of Professor Thatcher's feet tied to the chair flashed through Myrtle's mind.

"What about them?" she asked.

"Like I said, my Herbert, he's a fisherman. Dey said dat Mr. Thatcher and his son, dey was fishermen, too. I don't tink no self respectin' fisherman would've ever tied up dat man's legs usin' bows—you know, like on a package, or when you tie your shoelaces like in da book?

"Fishermen know knots; dey would've used a fisherman's knot to tie his legs up wit—not a bow."

Myrtle's eyes lit up. *That* was what had baffled her when she looked at the photos that she hadn't been able to put her finger on—the way Professor Thatcher's legs were tied to the chair!

I have to get home right away and tell Henri.

"You find anything?" asked George, coming through the door.

"Did I ever!" said Myrtle. "George, you have to take me back to the boarding house right now. Wait—first, Paige, I want you to sign one of your books for me.

"And Mrs. Cardiff—thanks. You've been a great help."

*****

"I admit it raises questions," said Henri when Myrtle confronted him with the news she'd discovered. "But I don't know what's to be done about it. They were found guilty—that's it."

"Maybe a new trial," said Myrtle. "Couldn't the judge order a new trial? I mean, now we know—or at least we're pretty sure that Professor Thatcher did send his brother a note and in all likelihood he and Lincoln did spend the night at the cabin. And now, this new piece of evidence that seems to show someone else other than the Thatchers tied up the professor. Surely that's enough to raise some questions."

"What you're forgetting," said Henri, "is the rest of the evidence. The knife from the set in the workshop was found in Orville's shed along with the clothesline. There was blood on the knife. There's the note the professor left for you; he seemed sure Orville was out to get him. And then there's the insurance policy."

"That Mr. Thatcher said he never saw and knew nothing about."

"And the application on which he admitted was his signature."

Myrtle didn't say anything for a long time.

Finally, she said, "I'm going to bed. I have to give this more thought."

CHAPTER THIRTY-ONE

People still talked about the mother bear who led her cubs down Booker Falls' main street back in 1907.

It was mid-January, a time when most bears were in their winter dens, waiting for spring, when their food sources—grasses, roots, berries, acorns, nuts, and insects—once again became more available. Streams and ponds were frozen over, restricting the animal's access to water to drink and fish to eat.

But bears don't really hibernate—they're in a state of torpor, which means they're only asleep. Sometimes on mild winter days they will awaken and sally forth in search of food. Apparently, that was the case with that bear because, with her two cubs waddling behind, she'd made a beeline for the wooden bin behind J. P. Finnegan's Fancy Groceries and Fresh Meats where Mr. Finnegan dumped his garbage until it was picked up on Tuesday's and Saturdays by Milford Whitman, who then transported it to his farm to feed his pigs.

This particular day was a Friday, which meant there was a good three days' worth of good eatin's in the bin—good eatin's for bears, that is.

The townsfolk watched—at a safe distance—as mama bear and the cubs gorged themselves, then curled up next to the back of the building for a short nap. Thirty minutes later they were gone, back to their den for the remainder of the winter, as they never showed up again.

The next time a bear played a role in the town proved more disastrous when a year ago one attacked a young woman, one of the students at the college. Only the brave actions of Claude Amyx, the school custodian, had saved her.

A dwarf, barely four-foot-four and weighing no more than one hundred and fifty pounds, Claude killed the bear with only a knife, sustaining serious wounds that took him months from which to recover in the process.

Since then everything had been quiet—bear-wise.

Until now.

"Henri, Henri!"

Henri looked up to see Andy Erickson dashing into his office.

"What is it?" asked Henri, getting up from his desk. "What's happened?"

"It's Louis Mullineaux—he got mauled by a bear! Ya gotta come quick!"

Henri strapped on his revolver, then reached into the corner and picked up his rifle.

"Where is he?" he asked, hurrying out the door.

"Who, the bear?"

"No, Louis. Is somebody looking after him?"

"Yah," said Andy, "Winnie Pulkkinen went and got Doc Sherman. He's probly on his way there now."

"And this happened over at the Pulkkinen place?"

"Yah."

"What about the bear?" asked Henri.

"Marvin said it run off in the woods."

Henri jumped into his car. "Was Marvin with Louis when it happened?"

"Nah," said Andy, jumping into the car alongside Henri. "He heard him screamin' and run out of his barn just in time to see da bear skedaddlin'. He called his wife to go get da doc and he's wit Louis now."

"How'd you learn all this?" asked Henri, starting the car and pulling out into the street.

"I was over at Doc's havin' him look at a cut I got when Winnie come runnin' in. Doc sent me to get you."

Fifteen minutes later, Henri pulled the car to a stop at the Pulkkinen farm.

"Doc!" he shouted as he jumped out of the car.

"Back here," came the doctor's voice from behind the barn.

Henri, with Andy following close behind, ran around the barn and found Doctor Sherman kneeling over a mangled Louis Mullineaux, trying desperately to stop the bleeding. Winnie was on her knees, wiping blood from Louis's face while Marvin lingered nearby, watching helplessly.

"Henri, we have to get him to the hospital in Houghton," said Doctor Sherman without stopping in his efforts to staunch the bleeding. "Let's go in your car. My carriage would take too long."

"I'll bring the car around," said Henri, running back toward his vehicle.

Henri pulled the car to a stop a few feet from where everyone was gathered and jumped out.

Doctor Sherman was on his feet, hands at his side.

"Too late," he said. "He's gone."

"What was Louis doing out here?" asked Henri, turning to Winnie and Marvin.

"He liked to come out to walk," said Winnie. "You know,

dis used to be his home place 'til we bought it."

"He wasn't hunting or anything?" asked Henri.

"Nah," said Marvin. "I don't tink old Louis even owned a gun no more."

"You think this might be the same bear that got Pinky Richardson's pigs last week?" asked Doctor Sherman.

Henri nodded. "Might be. If we have a bear that kills pigs and attacks a man for no reason, then we've got a problem. I reckon I need to get the D.O.C. involved in this."

"What's the D.O.C.?" asked Marvin.

"Department of Conservation," said Henri.

"Andy, you help me get Louis's body in my carriage, will you?" said Doctor Sherman.

"And I advise the two of you to keep an eye out for that bear," said Henri, speaking to Marvin and Winnie. "I wouldn't let any of my smaller animals be running loose, either."

"Hell," said Andy as he helped the doctor with Louis's body, "I wouldn't let none of my animals run loose, big or small, not wit a wild bear runnin' 'round."

*****

The bear attack on Louis Mullineaux was the topic of conversation at the dinner table that evening. Myrtle was there for a change as she had caught a cold the night of Paige's book signing and had stayed home from the library.

"What are you going to do about the bear?" asked Pierre.

"Are we safe being out?" asked Daisy.

"I think as long as you're in town you're okay," said Henri. "And as far as the bear is concerned—I'm going to track it down and kill it."

Everyone sat, stunned at what Henri just said. *He* was going to kill the bear?

Myrtle set down the glass of milk from which she was

about to take a drink. "I thought you called that state office."

"The Department of Conservation," said Henri. "I did. I talked to a Mr. Young there. He said they didn't have any conservation officers in this area right now, and if I thought the bear was an imminent threat to the community I should go ahead and dispose of it myself. He authorized me to do so."

"Henri, that sounds awfully dangerous," said Myrtle. The concern on her face was evident. "Do you even know how to track a bear . . . or any animal, for that matter?"

"Nah, I never was much of a woodsman. But I have somebody who is."

"Who's that?" asked Daisy.

"Grissom."

"Who's Grissom?" asked Daisy.

"Wait;" said Myrtle, "isn't he the Indian Mr. Murphy attacked on the street that day?"

"That's him," said Henri. "I told Andy what I had to do and he said he knew Grissom, that that was how he made what little money he did, by tracking and trapping animals for their pelts. I reminded Andy that what Grissom was doing was probably against the law."

"What did he say to that?" asked Myrtle.

"He said since Grissom was an Indian he was pretty sure he was allowed to hunt and trap as much as he wanted to, since most of it was on Indian land to start with. He also said he was sure I could probably handle a three or four-hundred-pound bear on my own."

"I told him to have Grissom come and see me," said Henri when the laughing stopped. "I told Andy I may be dumb, but I'm not stupid."

CHAPTER THIRTY-TWO

"So, what do you think?" asked Henri.

Grissom had met Henri at the Pulkkinen farm. Grissom was down on his knees, studying the bear prints. Perched next to him on his haunches was what appeared to be a wolf.

"What I tink," said Grissom, as he stood up, "is dat you got a rogue bear on your hands here, Constable. And tings ain't gonna get any better wit him around. He's got to go."

"That's what I thought," said Henri. "So, can you track him?"

Grissom looked at Henri and grinned. "Constable, *you* could track dis bear. Question is: what you gonna do wit him when you find him? You gonna kill him or trap him and move him someplace else?"

Henri didn't speak for a minute. He hadn't considered the latter option.

"What do you think?" he asked finally.

"Oh, he gotta be killed," said Grissom. "Ain't gonna be nothin' but trouble no matter where he is."

Henri nodded. "All right, then, let's go find him. I have to say, your dog looks more like a wolf than a dog."

"Dat's 'cause he's half wolf."

"But he's tame?" asked Henri.

Grissom grinned. "As tame as a half-wolf can be."

"What's his name?"

"Maji-manidoo," said Grissom.

"Is that Ojibwe?" asked Henri.

"Yah."

"What's it mean?"

"Devil," said Grissom.

"Uh, huh," said Henri, moving back a step. "Okay, I'll go round up some more help; be back shortly."

"Ain't no need for more help;" said Grissom, "only slow us down."

"You think you and I are all we need?" asked Henri.

Grissom smiled. "I jus' bringin' you along for da company, Constable . . . and to help me carry back da meat and da pelt."

Henri laughed. "Well, okay, then, let's get to it."

*****

Though spring had technically made its appearance over a month earlier, the forest floor was still covered by a good foot of snow, making it easy to track the bear.

Henri had spent the first seventeen years of his life in French Guiana which, like Michigan, was canopied with trees —but not like those under which he now followed in Grissom's tracks. Here he was surrounded by beech and poplar, maple and pine. His homeland had trees with exotic sounding names like pau-rosa, minquartia, astrocaryum, and mahogany. He smiled, remembering that when he first arrived in Michigan the names of the trees had sounded exotic to him.

He stopped for a moment to listen. But all he heard was silence—a silence so profound it seemed to wrap itself around him, making it feel as though time itself had paused in its normal inexorable forward movement.

He watched Grissom plodding along in front of him, the snow so powdery his snowshoes made no noise. It was as if he were walking on air.

The trees, usually bustling with the sounds of squirrels and birds, stood quiet.

Henri shook his head. Enough daydreaming.

He started off, hurrying to catch up with Grissom. He had almost reached him when Grissom stopped and held up one hand.

"The bear?" whispered Henri.

Grissom shook his head and pointed.

Henri looked in the direction Grissom had pointed and saw what appeared to be a deer . . . or was it an elk? He wasn't sure.

"What *is* that?" he whispered to Grissom.

"Gray ghost," Grissom whispered back.

"Gray—?"

The animal looked in their direction, then quickly disappeared behind a towering oak.

"Caribou," said Grissom. "It was a caribou. They're called Gray Ghosts because dey're so rarely seen. If we weren't out here for dat bear we'd be trackin' *it* right now."

"It was magnificent," said Henri.

"True it is," said Grissom. "Come, let's move on."

*****

An hour later they came to a stream that had rid itself of the ice that had covered it for the last five months. Grissom waded across while Henri waited on the bank.

Henri watched Grissom walk up one side of the bank then back down, searching the ground for any sign of the bear.

"I tink we got a pretty smart bear," he said, finally.

"What do you mean?"

"Dat bear didn't cross here. He either went upstream or

down. I don't know which. We'll have to check out both directions."

"Should we split up?" asked Henri.

He realized as soon as the words were out of his mouth how absurd they were; even if he could track a bear as Grissom had said, would he be able to bring it down?

"No, I tink we stay together," said Grissom. "Better dat way."

"Yah, you're right," said Henri. He breathed a sigh of relief he hadn't been called out on his dumb suggestion.

"Dis way; let's head dis way," said Grissom, taking off upstream.

Henri followed on the opposite shore.

"I showed you his prints earlier," said Grissom. "I don't tink he would cross back over on your side but keep your eyes open all da same."

Thirty minutes later they came to a waterfall crashing down over a ledge some fifteen feet above them, creating a swirling pond at the bottom about twenty feet across.

"You see anyting over dere?" asked Grissom, shouting to be heard over the sound of the cascading water.

"Nah," Henri shouted back. "You?"

"Nah," shouted Grissom, shaking his head. He waved, an indication to Henri to head back downstream.

"I don't tink he came dis way," he said, once they were far enough away from the roar of the falls to make himself heard. "He must have headed downstream. We'll check dat out."

Two hours later, dusk was settling in. There was still no trace of the bear.

"We need to stop for da night," said Grissom. "Dis be a good place to set up camp."

*****

"So you're Objiwe?" asked Henri.

Grissom had set a fire, and he and Henri were indulging themselves in the pasties Mrs. Darling had sent with them, along with some homemade lemon cookies.

"Yah," Grissom answered. "I was born on da reservation."

"The L'Anse reservation."

"Yah, dat one. Left dere when I was eighteen. I got work at loggin' camps around da area, providin' dem wit fresh meat dat I hunted and trapped. Did some fur tradin', too. Now I mostly just trap and sell furs. Ain't much, but it keeps me in food."

"Where do you live—in town?"

"Nah. Me and Niimi got a little shack outside town."

"You're married?" asked Henri.

"Oh, yah, ten years now. Got two kids. How about you, Constable—you married?"

"Hoping to be," said Henri, grinning.

"You got a girl, den?"

"Myrtle…Myrtle Tully. I've asked her to marry me."

"Oh, yah," said Grissom. "She say yes?"

Henri scrunched up his face. "Not yet—but she will."

"She be good wife for you."

"Do you know her?" asked Henri.

"Everybody know Miss Tully. 'Sides, she offered to help me when dat Declan guy was trying to beat me."

"Right," said Henri. "I'd forgotten about that."

"Good ting you come along when you did."

"Oh, I don't think Declan would have seriously hurt you."

"Nah," said Grissom, grinning. "I not da one who was in danger. If dat white man not come along—"

"Professor Thatcher."

"Yah, I guess dat's his name. If he not come along I would have killed dat Declan."

Henri stared at Grissom. He had no doubt he would have.

"We going to find that bear tomorrow?" he asked.

"Yah, you betcha. But now let's get some sleep; get early start tomorrow."

CHAPTER THIRTY-THREE

A quarter of a mile downstream from where they had camped, Henri and Grissom discovered where the bear had left the stream.

"Dis not good," said Grissom.

"No," said Henri. "He came back out on the same side he went in—he might be heading back toward town."

Grissom nodded. "Dat what I tink, too. Come on—we got to hurry, catch up wit him."

Shortly after two in the afternoon, they came upon what remained of a fawn. Grissom removed one glove, bent down and touched the blood. He knelt and smelled the fawn's body. Then he got to his feet.

"Da bear did dis," he said.

"I thought bears ate berries and leaves and such," said Henri.

"Yah, dat's true. But in da spring, dey need some meat. Dey'll even eat dead animals. Dis deer wasn't dead, dough—da bear killed it."

*****

Mrs. Darling picked up the cup of tea she'd just prepared

and took a sip. Then she leaned back in her chair and sighed.

She didn't look forward to the walk into town. But today was Friday, which meant fish for dinner. She knew Mr. Finnegan would have some nice steelhead ready for her, or perhaps some salmon. Her mouth watered at the prospect. Normally she would ask Henri to pick it up and bring it back for her, but he had gone out yesterday after that rogue bear with Grissom and hadn't come home last night. Daisy was working at the newspaper office, Myrtle was at the library, and Pierre had classes all day.

When Henri hadn't shown up last evening, Myrtle had worried something had happened to him, but Mrs. Darling assured her he was in good hands with Grissom.

"Dat Indian, he knows dose woods backwards and forwards," she'd said. "Dey just campin' out 'til daylight come. Den dey go get dat bear."

In truth, she'd felt some concern herself but managed not to let Myrtle see it.

Right now she was more concerned about dinner.

She heard a scratching at the door. She turned and saw Penrod standing there, an imploring look on his face.

"You got to go out again? You was just out ten minutes ago. Okay," she said, getting up and walking over to the door.

She opened it and the dog made a beeline for the mulberry tree, his favorite place to relieve himself.

Mrs. Darling started back for her tea when a torrent of barking exploded from the yard. What she saw when she stopped and looked back brought a knot to her stomach: a bear was lumbering toward Penrod, who was standing his ground, barking for all he was worth.

She felt her heart begin to beat faster and faster.

"Penrod!" she shouted.

But he paid her no mind. His attention was fixed on the

huge creature in front of him.

Mrs. Darling watched in horror as the bear suddenly lunged and grabbed Penrod up in his huge paws. The dog began squealing in terror.

Mrs. Darling ran to the pantry, grabbed the rifle Eugene brought back with him from his time serving in the Civil War, took a bullet from the box on the shelf and loaded the gun, then stuck another bullet into the pocket of the apron she wore. By the time she got back to the kitchen door, the bear was trudging away toward the woods, a yelping Penrod securely in its grasp.

The lungs. She remembered Eugene saying that the best place to shoot a bear to kill it was its lungs. But the bear was heading away from her. Could she shoot accurately enough to hit its lungs? And would a bullet penetrate far enough through the bear's back? If it went all the way through would it hit the dog?

It had been twelve years since she last shot this gun. Would it blow up in her face? Could she even hit the bear at all? She had to at least try.

She needed to get closer. She ran out about twenty yards into the yard, stopped, lifted the rifle, took aim, and fired. The sound was deafening; the recoil knocked her backward…but not down.

She watched as the bear stopped and shook its massive head.

I must have hit it, she thought. But where?

She watched as the bear slowly turned, dropped Penrod to the ground, then came charging at her. She reached into her pocket, her hand shaking, pulled the bullet out, slipped it into the breech, and fired again.

This time the bear stopped in its tracks and shook its head. Then, in what seemed like slow motion, it turned and staggered back toward the woods, crumpling to the ground a few yards from the tree line.

Penrod, who had been running around like a tornado looking for a place to set down, stopped, looked in the direction of Mrs. Darling, then raced to the safety of her arms. With one arm she scooped him up and hurriedly retreated to the safety of the house.

The bear was down.

But was it dead?

She wasn't about to find out.

Still holding the shaking Penrod in one arm and the rifle in her free hand, she ran into the house and down the hallway, depositing both the dog and the gun on the way. She lifted the telephone mouthpiece, tucked it under her chin, and turned the crank three times.

"Hey there, Rebecca, how you doin' today?" came the cheery voice of Maribel, the town's operator.

"No time for chitchat," said Mrs. Darling. "Give me Henri's office."

"Okey, dokey, will do," said Maribel.

"Teddy Simpson," came the voice on the other end of the line.

"Teddy, dis is Mrs. Darling. I just shot a bear but I don't know if he's dead or not."

There was dead silence.

Then, from the phone, "You shot a bear?"

"Yah, I shot a bear. I need you to come out here and make sure it's dead."

"Where's the bear now?" asked Teddy.

"In da back yard. I'm hopin' it's still dere."

"It's not moving?"

"Not the last time I looked."

"I'll be right there," said Teddy.

*****

Fifteen minutes later, Mrs. Darling watched through the kitchen window as Teddy drove into the backyard. She hurried out as he left the carriage. While she was waiting for him, she'd kept an eye on the bear through the window—it hadn't moved.

"Jesus, Joseph, and Mary, you weren't kidding!" exclaimed Teddy, studying the bear, all the while keeping a safe distance from it. He pulled his gun from its holster and cautiously approached the figure lying prostrate on the ground. He paused long enough to grab the pole that held up the clothesline. Six feet from the bear he stopped and, holding the pole at its very end, poked the animal in one eye.

There was no movement.

He poked the bear's eye again, this time more forcefully.

Still, no movement.

"I think you got him," Teddy said. "I think you got him. He's dead."

"Tank God," said Mrs. Darling, putting one hand to her heart that was still beating wildly. "What do we do wit him now?"

"If Henri and Grissom are still tracking him, they'll show up here eventually . . . probably pretty soon. Grissom will skin and dress him. In the meantime, keep your dog away from him."

Mrs. Darling laughed. "I'm pretty sure Penrod don't want nothin' to do wit dat bear now."

*****

"This isn't good," said Henri.

It was clear to him and Grissom that the bear was heading in the direction of the boarding house. Mrs. Darling would be there by herself.

"Hurry," he said, increasing his stride.

Twenty minutes later, they emerged from the woods behind the barn.

"Holy wah!" cried Grissom when they saw the bear.

"Is it dead?" Henri asked Teddy, who was standing nearby.

"Yah, it's dead all right."

"Who killed it? You?"

"Dat would be me."

Henri and Grissom turned to see Mrs. Darling bouncing out from the house, grinning broadly. "I can tell you who killed dat bear. It was me! *I* killed dat bear."

"You?" said Henri, a shocked look on his face. "*You* killed the bear?"

"Dat's right," said Mrs. Darling.

"How?" asked Henri, still not believing that this small woman could have brought down a three-hundred-pound bear.

"Shot him to death," said Mrs. Darling.

"Henri, come help me roll him over," said Grissom.

When the bear was lying on its back, it was Grissom who was smiling.

"You shot him right in da left lung," he said. "And, in da neck. Dat's perty good shootin'."

"Pretty lucky shooting," said Henri. "That bear could have killed you."

"He had Penrod," said Mrs. Darling. "And it wasn't 'pretty good' shootin'. Well, da first shot was—da one to da neck. But when he turned 'round back toward me, I knew den where I had to put da next shot . . . right where my Eugene told me it had to be."

"Who?" asked Grissom.

"Eugene—my late husband. He told me once where to shoot a bear if you want to kill it. I remembered. 'Sides, I couldn't afford to miss—I din't have no more bullets left."

*****

The talk that evening, not only at the boarding house dining room table but all over town, was how Mrs. Darling had brought down the bear. Daisy had come home early from the newspaper office to take pictures with her Kodak of Mrs. Darling standing next to the creature, which Grissom and Henri had tied upright against the barn wall.

"Mrs. Darling," said Myrtle, as they all sat in the parlor enjoying hot chocolate, "no one is ever going to think about messing around with you anymore."

"I'll drink to that," said Pierre.

Everybody lifted their glass.

"To Mrs. Darling," they all said.

"Bear slayer," added Daisy. "Davey Crockett has nothing on you, Mrs. Darling."

CHAPTER THIRTY-FOUR

Myrtle caressed the watch that she wore on a silver chain around her neck, a birthday gift from everyone at the boarding house. The front of the case displayed a floral design, while on the back in a fancy script, were her engraved initials: *MET*.

She flipped open the lid, revealing a pink pearlized face and the word *Lucerne*. The time was 4:27. She shook her head, walked over to one of the glass windows in her office, and glanced up at the large Ansonia clock on the wall: 4:29. She walked back to her desk and flopped down in her chair.

She couldn't believe it wasn't yet six o'clock.

Game night was on tap this evening at the boarding house. Daisy had suggested it, and both Henri and Pierre jumped at the chance. There was no question Myrtle was in; she was an avid game player, especially board games, and had acquired a reputation as a zealous competitor.

Fortuitously, Mrs. Darling kept an extensive collection of games in the hall closet that she had collected over the years for the enjoyment of her tenants, among them The Checkered Board Game of Life, Parcheesi, Mansion of Happiness,

Banking, The Landlord's Game, and——Myrtle's favorite——Round The World With Nellie Bly.

It was the latter which was on the agenda this evening.

On November 14, 1889, Elizabeth Cochrane Seaman, an American journalist better known by her pen name, Nellie Bly, set off on an around the world trip to emulate the journey taken by the character, Phileas Fogg, in Jules Verne's novel, *Around the World in Eighty Days*, written some seventeen years before. The trip was financed by the *New York World* newspaper.

Nellie was successful in her quest and returned to New York on January 25, 1890. When the board game came out later that year, Mrs. Darling bought one of the first sets.

When six o'clock rolled around, Myrtle grabbed her coat and rushed out of the library, leaving one of the seniors whom she trusted to lock up the place.

Henri waited in his car at the end of the path.

"Let's go!" cried Myrtle, as she jumped in.

Henri put his foot on the gas pedal and off they sped.

Normally, Mrs. Darling would have a warm meal—soup or casserole—waiting for Myrtle when she got home from the library. Tonight, though, at Myrtle's request she had prepared a turkey and cheese sandwich and an apple, food Myrtle could eat while playing.

"Hurry up, Myrtle," said Daisy as her housemate ran through the hallway to the kitchen. "The game's all set up. We're ready to play."

Myrtle set her plate and glass of milk on the table, pulled out her chair, and sat down.

"First of all," she said, "I want to say how sorry I am."

"Sorry for what?" asked Pierre.

"That I'm going to beat all of you so badly tonight,"

Myrtle answered with a laugh.

"Yah, we'll see about that," said Henri.

*****

By eight o'clock it was evident Myrtle was right—she was trouncing them badly.

"I don't know how you do it," said a frustrated Daisy, watching as Myrtle landed in San Francisco; it was the sixty-ninth day of Nellie's trip.

Two plays later, Myrtle won the game.

"I thought you were in real danger there in Singapore," said Pierre.

"Me, too," said Myrtle.

"Do you suppose Mr. Pulitzer took out an insurance policy on Nellie?" asked Pierre.

"Mr. Pulitzer?" said Daisy. "What did he have to do with it?"

"Mr. Pulitzer owned the newspaper that sponsored Nellie's trip," said Myrtle.

"Ah," said Daisy. "But could he do that? Take out an insurance policy on someone else, I mean?"

"Oh, it's done all the time," said Pierre. "The party to be insured has to agree to it. Otherwise, someone who's unscrupulous could purchase a policy on someone and then have them done away with."

Myrtle sat still for a moment, as myriad thoughts ran through her mind. Suddenly, she jumped up from her chair.

"That's it," she said. "That's how we can know for sure!"

"Know for sure what?" asked a startled Daisy.

"Pierre, would you please be so kind as to put the game away?" said Myrtle. "I need to talk with Daisy."

CHAPTER THIRTY-FIVE

Daisy settled back into the soft seat of Myrtle's Model N and let the cool breeze flow over her face. April was almost gone and with it the last vestiges of winter.

Daisy had been enticed by her housemate to accompany her on a trip to Hancock. Myrtle even offered to buy her lunch at Marinucci's Restaurant in Houghton, where she had previously dined with Henri.

"What's so special about Hancock that we need to go there?" Daisy had asked her the previous evening when Myrtle asked her to go.

"Because the game is afoot," said Myrtle. "That's where Professor Thatcher's doctor's office and the office that issued the insurance policy on him are."

"The game is afoot, huh? Didn't Sherlock Holmes say that?"

"He did," said Myrtle. "But he wasn't the first."

"No? Who then?"

"William Shakespeare."

"These offices—are they both open on Sunday?" asked Daisy.

"No, but I called the gentlemen and they agreed to meet with me," Myrtle replied. "Daisy, I've been wondering—are you going to keep on working at the newspaper after you and Eddie get married?"

Daisy looked at Myrtle. "I guess so. Why wouldn't I?"

"Do you love your job?"

"I wouldn't say *love*," answered Daisy. "It's an okay job. I get to write, which is what I want to do."

"You were going to write a novel about Mr. Pfrommer."

Daisy sighed. "Yeah. That's not going to happen. I've decided I'm not a novelist. I'm not very good at making things up. How about you? You going to stay on at the library after you're married?"

"What makes you think I'm getting married?"

"Because I can tell you're ready."

Myrtle laughed. "Ready, huh? I don't know about that."

"I do," said Daisy. "So, *if* you get married, are you staying on at the library?"

"I've been thinking about that."

"And?"

"I'm not sure."

"What else would you do?"

"Maybe become a Pinkerton agent…or a female detective."

Daisy's jaw dropped. "A Pinkerton agent? A female detective?"

"Yes, you remember last year—Kitty Vanderliet?"

"The Pinkerton agent who saved your life?"

"I wouldn't exactly say she saved my life," said Myrtle.

"When she came upon you and that Mr. Hutchinson in the cave under the library and you tried to defend yourself with a statue and he had a gun?"

"Yeah, okay, maybe she did save my life. Anyway, I've

been wondering what it would be like to be a Pinkerton agent like her. I do like to solve crimes, you know."

"Yes, you do," Daisy agreed. "And I have to admit—you are pretty good at it."

"Thank you," said Myrtle. "That's what I thought, too."

"But why Pinkerton?"

"Because they value their female agents. Did you ever hear of Kate Warne?"

Daisy shook her head. "Can't say that I have."

"She was the first female agent Pinkerton ever hired. She even helped thwart an attempt to assassinate President Lincoln."

"She did? How'd she do that?"

"First of all she went undercover and got in with the plotters; then she helped smuggle the president onto a train to get him out of harm's way."

"Sounds like quite a woman," said Daisy.

Myrtle nodded. "I'd like to do something like that."

*****

Entering Houghton, they passed the college as they approached the downtown area.

"You didn't go to college, did you?" asked Daisy.

"Nope, only high school."

"You're smart enough to have gone to college. Wish I could have."

Myrtle smiled. "Thank you. I think you're pretty smart, too."

"Remember when we came here to go out to Electric Park?" asked Daisy spotting the Douglas House, Houghton's finest hotel. "Right there's where we caught the trolley."

"As I recall, that was the day Eddie proposed to you," said Myrtle.

"It sure was," said Daisy, a big smile on her face. "Which

brings us back to our previous topic and to my next question: when are you going to make up your mind?"

"My mind about what?" asked Myrtle, teasingly.

"About who the lucky guy is going to be," said Daisy. "Who are you going to walk down the aisle with? When are you going to decide?"

"Well, if you must know—I already have," said Myrtle looking straight ahead.

"What?" exclaimed Daisy. "When were you going to tell me?"

"Today—on this trip. At lunch."

"Huh-uh, I need to know right now. I don't want to wait 'til lunch. Pull over—pull over now!"

Myrtle pulled the car to the sidewalk and parked.

"What now?" she asked in an innocent tone.

"You're going to tell me who you're going to marry or we're not budging from this spot."

"Oh, okay," said Myrtle, grinning. "But you'll have to lean closer so I can whisper it to you."

"Whisper it to me? Why do you have to whisper? Who's going to hear you? And aren't you going to let it out soon, anyway?"

"The whole world will hear if I say it out loud."

"What do you mean 'the whole world will hear'"?

"James Hutton, the eighteenth-century geologist believed the whole earth was like a living organism; it could breathe and hear just as we humans can."

"Balderdash!" Daisy exploded. She sank back in her seat.

Not a word from Myrtle.

"Okay, whisper," said Daisy, leaning back up and toward Myrtle.

Myrtle leaned over and whispered a name.

"Darn," said Daisy, sinking back into the seat.

"Darn?" said Myrtle. "That's all you can say is 'darn'?"

"Oh, well, yes, I'm excited for you. It's just that I'm not going to win the two dollars I had counted on."

"Two dollars?"

"Yeah, Pierre and I have a bet on who you'd choose. I didn't guess the right guy."

"Now I suppose you owe Pierre two dollars?" said Myrtle.

"No," said Daisy. "He didn't pick the right guy either. What did he say when you said 'yes'?"

"I haven't told him yet. You remember I told you you'd be the third to know? You're actually the second—right after me."

Daisy looked surprised. "You haven't said yes to him?"

Myrtle shook her head.

"What if he's changed his mind?"

Now it was Myrtle's turn to look surprised.

"Changed his mind? Why would he have changed his mind?"

"Maybe he got tired of waiting. Oh, well, no problem—you still have a backup...or two."

"No, no, no!" cried Myrtle. "He's not allowed to change his mind!"

"If I were you I wouldn't wait another second. As soon as we get back to town you better tell him."

"Well, okay, then," said Myrtle. "I will."

"One more question. How's that going to work—being a Pinkerton agent and a married woman?"

Myrtle was quiet for a minute. "Not sure. We'll have to see. I just might open a detective agency in Booker Falls. Now can we go on?"

"No, turn the car off."

"Turn the car off? What for?"

"Don't you remember what's right up here on the corner

by the bridge?"

For a minute Myrtle didn't know what Daisy was talking about. Then a grin spread over her face.

"The candy store!" she said. "Yelps Candy Store!"

"Come on," said Daisy, scrambling out of the car. "Let's go buy some Jujyfruits!"

*****

Thirty minutes later, after filling three bags with Peach Blossoms, peppermint sticks, Hershey's milk chocolate Kisses, Goo Goo Clusters, Mary Janes, Turtles, and Brach's wrapped caramels they were on their way again, crossing the bridge over the Portage River from Houghton into Hancock.

"The first time I saw this bridge I couldn't figure out how those bigger ships went under it," said Daisy. "Then I saw how it worked; how it disengaged from each end and swung around in the middle so the boats could pass on either side. Pretty neat."

"Yes, in New Orleans they build them high enough for the boats to pass under. Of course, the Mississippi is a little wider than the Portage."

"You think they'll ever build a bridge between the two peninsulas?" asked Daisy.

"You mean here in Michigan?"

"Yeah, the Upper and Lower Peninsulas."

"I don't know," said Myrtle. "But if they do, it's going to have to be pretty long."

"Yeah, and I don't think it will be a swing bridge like this one."

"There's the building," said Myrtle. "I can park right here."

"You don't need me along for this," said Daisy. "While you're having your meetings I'm going to check out that little dress shop. Meet you back here at the car?"

"Okay," said Myrtle, taking off. "Then we'll go have lunch."

*****

"I was saddened when I got your phone call," said Dr. Järvinen. "I can't believe someone killed Professor Thatcher. He was such a gentle man. And his nephew was nice, too."

"You met Lincoln?"

"Oh, yes. He was with Mr. Thatcher when I gave him the bad news."

"And when was that?" asked Myrtle.

"A little over three months ago. He would probably have only lived another two or three months, had his life not been taken."

"Do you know if Professor Thatcher's brother knew? Orville?"

Dr. Järvinen shrugged. "I wouldn't know. I didn't tell him. Never met the man. Unless Professor Thatcher or his nephew told him, I wouldn't think so."

"Is there anything else you can tell me?" asked Myrtle.

Dr. Järvinen shook his head. "Not that I can think of. As I said, I never met the brother; but I can't believe the nephew had anything to do with the death. Professor Thatcher took the news of the seriousness of his condition quite well. His nephew actually broke down and cried. I believe he was truly fond of his uncle."

Myrtle stood to leave.

"By the way," said the doctor, "I have a sister who lives in Booker Falls—Hannah. She's the organist at St. Barbara's. Do you know her by any chance?"

A smile spread over Myrtle's face. "She's playing the organ for my wedding in a few weeks."

Thirty minutes later, after meeting with the insurance agent who sold the policy on the professor's life, Myrtle was back at the car. Soon Daisy appeared with a dress shop bag in each hand.

"Looks as though you were successful," said Myrtle.

"Wait 'til we get home and I can show you what I got," said Daisy. "How'd it go with the doctor and the insurance guy?"

"It was very informative. I'll tell you over lunch."

CHAPTER THIRTY-SIX

Henri and Jake sat in Judge Hurstbourne's office, wondering why they had been summoned.

"Do you know what this is all about?" asked Henri.

"Not a clue? You?"

"Nah. I just know he left a message with Mrs. Darling asking me to be here."

"I'm sure we'll find out," said Jake.

Both men jumped to their feet when the judge came through the door.

"Oh, relax, fellas; we ain't in court now," said the judge. "I'm sure you're curious as to why I asked you to meet here today."

"We were wondering," said Jake.

"Miss Tully phoned me and said she had some new information about the Thatcher case and wondered if she could meet with me and the two of you to discuss it."

"New information?" said Jake. "She does realize the case is over, and both men were found guilty?"

"And are already serving their sentences over in Marquette?" added Henri.

"I'm sure she does," said Judge Hurstbourne. "But I have a great deal of respect for Miss Tully, seeing as how she was instrumental in solving those three other murder cases. I told her I would hear her out . . . as I'm sure both of you are willing to do."

Neither Jake nor Henri was going to argue with Judge Hurstbourne about that.

Just then Myrtle appeared at the door.

"Miss Tully," said Judge Hurstbourne, jumping to his feet, followed closely by Jake and Henri. "Come in, come right on in."

"Good afternoon, gentlemen," said Myrtle as she settled into an empty chair.

"Judge Hurstbourne says you have some new information on the Thatcher case," said Jake.

The three men all took their seats.

"I do," said Myrtle. "And I think this information will show that Mr. Draper was right—that Mr. Thatcher *was* framed for the murder of his brother."

"Framed? By who?" asked Jake.

"And what about Lincoln?" asked Henri. "Was he framed also?"

"I'll get to all of that," said Myrtle.

She reached into the valise she was carrying, pulled out Paige's book and laid it on the judge's desk.

"First, let me show you why I don't believe either Mr. Thatcher or his son was involved in the murder."

"And this book will prove that?" asked Judge Hurstbourne. "This children's book?"

"In a way," said Myrtle. "Henri, you know there was something in the photographs Daisy took that didn't look right to me; but I couldn't put my finger on it."

"Yah," said Henri, "I remember you mentioning that."

"I finally figured out what it was."

"And this book helped you?" asked Jake.

"This and a conversation I had with Mrs. Cardiff."

"One of the jurors in the case?" said Jake.

"Yes," said Myrtle. "I met Mrs. Cardiff at Paige's book signing. She told me she was the one who kept the jury out for so long because she noticed something in one of the photos that bothered her. Unlike me, she knew what it was."

"What was that?" asked the judge.

Myrtle reached into her valise again and pulled out the photo of the professor's legs tied to the chair in which he sat.

"This," said Myrtle.

Jake looked at the photo and shrugged. "What about it?" he asked. "I don't see anything suspicious."

"Mrs. Cardiff's husband is a fisherman," said Myrtle. "When she saw the clothesline that was binding Professor Thatcher's legs had been tied in a bow, like one would use on a package, she thought that if Mr. Thatcher and Lincoln were also fishermen, they would have used different knots, fishermen's knots, instead of a bow. That's when I realized it was the same question I had. Well, sort of the same question."

"I can see where that might raise a question;" said Judge Hurstbourne, "but I hardly think it's conclusive."

"That's only part of it," said Myrtle, holding up the book. "This is a book about a little girl who couldn't tie her shoelaces because she was left-handed."

The men sat silent, wondering where Myrtle was going with this.

"The thing is," said Myrtle, "many left-handed people cannot tie their shoelaces because they never learned how—the laces go differently if you're right-handed. The reason they never learned how is because it's almost impossible for a right-handed person to teach a left-handed person how to tie a bow, how to tie shoelaces. Both Mr. Thatcher and Lincoln are left-handed; they never learned how to tie a bow, nor their shoelaces. Both of Mr. Thatcher's parents were right-handed as was Mr. Thatcher's wife, so neither he nor Lincoln had anyone who could show them how to tie a bow. When I talked to Mr. Thatcher on the phone—"

"When was that?" asked the judge.

"Last week. I called over to the prison and the warden let me speak with him. Anyway, he confirmed that neither he nor Lincoln ever learned how to tie shoelaces; that's why they only wore shoes or boots they could slip on or ones that had buckles. When I picked up the photograph at their house—"

"Photograph?" said Jake.

"At their house?" asked Henri.

"Yes, I'll get to that later. When I picked up the photograph I checked all their closets—there was no footwear that had shoelaces, only boots that slipped on or had buckles. If you look at the photo it's apparent the bow is tied like most people would tie it—by right-handed people. First of all, if either Mr. Thatcher or Lincoln tied the professor's legs they would almost undoubtedly have used a knot. But even had they used a bow, they couldn't possibly have tied these bows; they were definitely tied by someone who is right-handed."

"That's all very interesting," said Jake.

"And compelling," said Judge Hurstbourne, eliciting looks of surprise from both Jake and Henri.

"Do you have more?"

"I do, Your Honor. Nothing that can prove the innocence of Mr. Thatcher and Lincoln but enough to question their guilt."

"And what would that be?" asked Judge Hurstbourne.

Myrtle reached into her valise again and pulled out a slip of paper.

"Your Honor, I have a signed affidavit here from Walter Compton, a student at the college. It states that on the day Professor Thatcher was killed, he paid Mr. Compton two dollars to deliver an envelope to Mr. Thatcher's address. He was told to hand it directly to Mr. Thatcher, which he did."

"Did this Mr. Compton know what was in the envelope?" asked Henri.

"No," said Myrtle, "he did not. But I believe it was the note Mr. Thatcher says he received from his brother asking for a meeting at the cabin."

"But why would the professor have asked for that when he was expecting you at his home?" asked Henri.

"Exactly," said Myrtle. "And I'll get to that, too."

"You said you thought Mr. Draper was on the right trail when he brought up the possibility Mr. Thatcher had been framed," said Judge Hurstbourne. "Do you have any idea who might have done that?"

"I believe I know without a doubt," said Myrtle.

"And who might that be?" asked Jake, still not convinced.

"I believe the killer of Professor Edwin Thatcher was…"

Myrtle paused a minute to create a little more suspense.

"…Edwin Thatcher."

CHAPTER THIRTY-SEVEN

The three men sat for a moment, stunned by Myrtle's words.

Then Jake cried out. "What? You think the professor killed himself? That's preposterous!"

"And what brought you to that conclusion?" asked Judge Hurstbourne.

"First of all," said Myrtle, "is the motive. Professor Thatcher hated his brother for two reasons: first, that Mr. Thatcher stole the professor's girlfriend away from him and, second, that he was responsible for her death. The professor was still in love with her.

"Let me explain how I think the professor set this whole affair up to throw the blame on Mr. Thatcher. A little over three months ago he was informed by his doctor that he had terminal cancer, with only a short time to live. Here is an affidavit signed by his doctor, Dr. Järvinen, confirming that."

Myrtle placed the paper on the judge's desk. "On the day he died, the professor came to the library to check out a book, *Lessons on the Human Body.* When Henri and I searched his home the day after his death, I found the book and returned it to the library. A few days later when Lydia was putting it back in the stacks, she noticed a bookmark. It marked a page with an illustration of the human body. Lydia brought it to me because she saw that a pencil mark had been made, precisely where the heart would be. I now believe the professor made that mark to show exactly where the murder weapon should be inserted. After all, he would have only one shot at getting it right. That morning he also asked—practically insisted—that I come to his house that evening. I believe now it was so the time of death could be more firmly established.

"Later in the day, he called Mr. Compton in from the street to deliver the envelope. As I said, Mr. Compton was paid two dollars for this, a somewhat generous sum for such a small job. When Mr. Compton mentioned that to the professor he said to him, 'you can't take it with you.' He knew he would die that evening."

"But why did he want his brother to go to the cabin anyway?" asked Teddy.

"Two reasons," said Myrtle. "First, with Mr. Thatcher gone, it allowed the professor to have access to his home and shed to leave the evidence he wanted to plant. Secondly, he wanted his brother to be someplace where he couldn't provide a substantiated alibi."

All the men nodded.

"Later, after Mr. Compton had had time to deliver the envelope and the professor was sure his brother was on his way to the cabin, he went to Mr. Thatcher's home. That was who Mrs. Jones saw there: 'a man wearing glasses,' she said. When he went around to the back of the house he planted the knife in the shed and cut four pieces of the clothesline to take with him back to his workshop."

"How would he have known there would be clothesline there for him to use?" asked Jake.

"He wouldn't. But when Henri and I were in the barn I

saw a coil of thin rope hanging on one of the uprights. He might have planned to use that but realized when he saw the clothesline it would make better evidence."

"You say he left the knife," said Judge Hurstbourne. "But the knife had blood on it. When did that happen?"

"I think Professor Thatcher purposely cut himself before he left his workshop so the blood would be on the knife."

"That might explain the knife and the clothesline and the cut on his arm," said Henri. "And I emphasize the word 'might;' but how about the life insurance policy?"

"A stroke of genius on the professor's part;" said Myrtle, "and proof that he killed himself."

"Proof?" said the judge.

"On one of his trips to the doctor's office, Professor Thatcher must have noticed Mr. Karhu's insurance office in the same building. When he decided to take his own life and throw the blame on his brother, he needed to give him a motive—a better one than just being thrown out of the cabin. So the professor stopped at the insurance office and picked up an application. Mr. Karhu said he told the professor he could fill the application out right there in the office but he insisted on taking it home with him. I'm sure that was so he could forge Mr. Thatcher's signature. We found a letter in the professor's desk written and signed by Mr. Thatcher, sent to him when the professor told him to vacate the cabin. The professor was an excellent penman—he taught penmanship at the college. It would have been a simple matter to forge Mr. Thatcher's signature. Actually, not so simple since he was right-handed and Mr. Thatcher was left-handed, so there would have been some differences if the samples had been closely examined by a graphologist."

"But they weren't," said Jake. "What makes you think the professor purchased the policy and not Orville?"

"As I said earlier, when I stopped at Mr. Thatcher's home I checked on his and Lincoln's footwear. I also picked up a photograph from the mantle, a picture of Mr. Thatcher and Lincoln. When Daisy and I drove to Hancock I went to the insurance office after I'd seen Dr. Järvinen and met with Mr. Karhu. I showed him the photo. I had also taken a yearbook from the college along. I showed him the photo of Professor Thatcher from the book. Mr. Karhu confirmed it was the professor and not Orville Thatcher who had obtained the application and later came back and purchased the policy. He said when the professor stopped in the first time he——Mr. Harhu——was under the impression he was purchasing the policy on himself. But when Professor Thatcher said it was his brother, Orville, who was purchasing it, Mr. Karhu explained that the professor would have to sign an affidavit of agreement, that one cannot purchase a policy on another person without that person's approval. The professor wasn't too keen to do so, but finally he did. Here is Mr. Karhu's signed affidavit that corroborates everything I just told you."

Myrtle again reached into the valise, pulled out a sheet of paper, and laid it on the judge's desk.

"And here's a copy of the agreement that the professor signed."

Myrtle brought out a second sheet of paper and laid it on top of the previous sheet.

Judge Hurstbourne picked up both pieces of paper and read them. "It looks like you've been very thorough," he said.

"Thank you, Your Honor. And here's something I found interesting. Mr. Karhu said that when the professor signed the agreement, he never bothered to remove his glove."

Everyone stared at Myrtle. No one spoke.

"That would explain why the professor's fingerprints were not found on either the policy application or the policy itself,"

Myrtle continued. "He always kept his gloves on when he handled them."

"Are you sure?" asked Jake.

"I remember the first time the professor came into the library looking for a book on bees. When I asked him to write down the title of the book he kept his glove on."

"I can understand why he would have done it with the insurance papers if he wanted to avoid fingerprints," said Henri, "but why the book? Who wouldn't take their glove off to write something?"

"Someone who suffered from psoriasis," answered Myrtle. "Remember how scaly and white Professor Thatcher's hands were? I told you I thought it was psoriasis and Doctor Sherman confirmed it. The professor was evidently very self-conscious about it.

"And one last thing—I think Professor Thatcher left the message in his coat pocket for me to find—or for someone to find to give to me—that would point us in the direction of his brother as the suspect and a subsequent search of his home. I'm not sure there was enough of a reason to do so otherwise."

"Where does Lincoln fit into all this?" asked Henri.

"He was an innocent bystander. While he knew he was the sole beneficiary in his uncle's will, he also knew his uncle was dying of cancer. Professor Thatcher's doctor confirmed that Lincoln was in the room when he first told the professor. For him, it was only a matter of waiting until the professor died to get the money. He wouldn't have risked being caught by hurrying the process. And I believe something the professor didn't take into consideration was that Lincoln would go with his father to the cabin. He probably assumed Mr. Thatcher would drive there in his carriage or his sleigh. But he wouldn't have known that Mr. Thatcher no longer owned either; that he'd had to sell them because he needed the money. And, Lincoln told me the professor wasn't aware he was living with his father."

"This all sounds plausible," said Jake, "except for one thing. If the professor killed himself, what happened to the murder weapon—excuse me, the *weapon*, since you don't think it was murder. Where is it?"

Myrtle smiled mischievously. "That's the best part of all. There is no weapon."

The three men stared at her with blank looks.

Finally, Judge Hurstbourne spoke. "If there was no weapon, then how did the professor kill himself?"

"Oh, I didn't say there *wasn't* a weapon," said Myrtle. "I said there *isn't* a weapon—not anymore."

"Then how did the professor get rid of it?" asked Henri. "Doc Sherman said he would have died instantly."

Myrtle shrugged. "It just—" Myrtle threw her hands up in a gesture as if to ask 'who knows?'—"disappeared."

"Harrumph," said Jake. "Just disappeared, eh?"

"Here's what happened," said Myrtle. "When Henri and I inspected the scene of the so-called 'crime,' I saw the candle mold lying in the sink in a small puddle of water. I assumed the professor had washed the mold getting ready to make his candles. I was wrong.

"Sometime earlier that day or perhaps the previous evening he must have filled the molds with water from the pump in the workshop and set them outside the door. If you recall, that was during a time when the temperature never got above ten degrees and was often below zero at night. After arranging the scene in the workshop, Professor Thatcher removed his clothing other than his long johns and his slippers. He retrieved the candle mold that now contained eight icicles and removed one of them in the sink. He placed it on the towel on the table he had previously set next to the chair; that's why the towel was still damp. Then he quickly tied his legs with the clothesline—as though he were tying his shoes—and wrapped some more clothesline around his wrists as if they had been tied and he had escaped. He picked up the icicle from the table and plunged it into his heart.

"Doctor Sherman indicated he found a smudge of soot around the wound. I suspect the professor obtained the soot from the fireplace and marked the exact spot where he wanted to insert his 'weapon' based on the book from the library. He was successful and died instantly.

"Henri and I arrived within a half-hour after he died. By that time the icicle with which he killed himself had melted, which accounts for the moisture on his body and his long johns. You will recall, Henri, how ungodly hot the room was."

Henri nodded. "It sure was."

"And that, gentlemen," said Myrtle, sitting back in her chair, "was how Edwin Thatcher killed himself and framed his brother for the deed."

Again, nobody said anything for a few minutes before Judge Hurstbourne broke the silence.

"Miss Tully, do you have anything else to share with us?"

"No, Your Honor, that is all. But I hope it's sufficient to at least allow for enough reasonable doubt to order a new trial for Mr. Thatcher and Lincoln, both of whom I sincerely believe are innocent."

"I shall give this a great deal of thought overnight and let you know tomorrow what I have decided. And, Miss Tully, let me say—you do make a compelling argument."

A broad smile covered Myrtle's face. "Thank you, Your Honor."

*****

Henri and Jake watched Myrtle drive off.

"What do you think?" asked Henri.

"I'd hate to face off against her in court," said Jake, taking one of his Little Beauties from his coat pocket and lighting it.

*****

The ring of the telephone startled Myrtle, much as the bong of the grandfather clock at the boarding house used to. She didn't receive that many calls at her office in the library to make it a regular occurrence.

"Darn," she muttered, irritated by the interruption.

She jumped up and grabbed the earpiece from its cradle.

"Good morning, Myrtle," came the voice of Maribel, the operator. "I have Constable de la Cruz on the other end."

"Henri?" said Myrtle.

"Myrtle," said Henri, "I just got a call from Jake."

Myrtle held her breath. "And?" she said.

"The judge called him a few minutes ago. Looks like he bought your argument—he's decided to set aside the jury verdict. He's going to free Mr. Thatcher and Lincoln. They're going to be free men."

Myrtle grinned, clenched her fist, and pumped the air.

"Yes!" she exclaimed.

CHAPTER THIRTY-EIGHT

As was their normal Thursday evening routine, Myrtle found Henri waiting for her when she left the library after closing it.

"I'm looking forward to a nice glass of sherry when we get back to the boarding house," she said.

"How about a glass of scotch instead?"

Myrtle looked at him inquisitively.

"Jake wants us to come to his office to celebrate," said Henri.

"Celebrate? Celebrate what?"

"Mr. Thatcher and his son got back home today."

Myrtle beamed. "And only a week after Judge Hurstbourne decided to set aside the verdict!"

"Yah, a lot quicker than we anticipated."

"Then let's go," said Myrtle.

*****

"Myrtle, have you given any thought to leaving the library and starting your own detective agency?" asked Jake.

"It might pay better," said Myrtle, settling into the swivel chair at Jake's roll top desk. "And I could choose my own working hours."

"You'd be great at it," said Teddy.

"You said we were going to celebrate," said Myrtle, directing her remarks at Jake.

Jake brought a glass of scotch to Myrtle, then served the other three men who had found seats at the table. He walked back to the sideboard, picked up his glass, and turned to face them.

"To Miss Myrtle Tully, sleuth extraordinaire," he said, raising his glass.

Henri, George, and Teddy all raised their glasses.

"To Myrtle," said George and Henri.

"To Miss Tully," said Teddy.

"How about cigars all around?" asked Jake.

"Little Beauties," said Myrtle.

Jake looked at her in surprise. "You remember that, too?"

"They remind me of my father," said Myrtle. "I shall pass but by all means, please, all of you, feel free to light up. I quite enjoy the aroma."

Once the cigars had been passed around, they were all lit.

Teddy took one puff and started coughing uncontrollably.

"You ever smoke before?" asked Jake.

Unable to speak, Teddy just shook his head, continuing to cough.

Finally, he managed to stop. His eyes were watering and he was out of breath.

"Sorry 'bout that," he managed to get out, still gasping for air.

"I talked to the Thatchers today," said George. "And, Myrtle, I have the paperwork ready for you to execute the will. Mr. Thatcher plans to sell the house in Greytown and he and Lincoln will move into the cottage."

"What about the cabin?" asked Jake. "Are either of them going back to fishing?"

"No," said George. "Orville feels he's too old. And Lincoln said he might try to take over the professor's beekeeping pastime, make honey and candles. Said he enjoyed it when he was helping his uncle. He's going to ask Mrs. Redman to help him with the bees."

"That's nice," said Myrtle, "but I doubt it will be much of a money-making proposition."

"No worry," said George. "Professor Thatcher was very frugal. He left a sizable estate, enough to pay off Lincoln's debt to Joker and provide a nice income for some time to come. And the cottage is free of debt."

"What about the insurance?" asked Henri. "Will the insurance company pay the ten thousand dollars to Orville?"

"No," said George. "They said the policy was obtained fraudulently since the professor signed Orville's name. If he had signed his own name as the purchaser, it would have been honored. They did say they would refund the premium to Professor Thatcher's estate, so Lincoln will get the benefit of that. They both said they owed you their lives and when they get settled in they want you over for dinner."

"I'm just happy justice was done," said Myrtle.

"As am I," said Jake. "And this was one case I was happy to lose."

"I can't stop thinking about the blood on the knife," said Myrtle.

"What about it?" asked Henri.

"Well, we've arrived at a point where we can identify different types of blood and match those types to different individuals."

"So?" said Teddy.

"Why can't we be more specific? Why can't we match not only the type but the blood itself to a particular person? We know now that there are not two sets of fingerprints alike, that everyone's prints are specific to just one individual. Why not blood?"

"We can see the lines on fingerprints," said Henri. "But with blood, all we see is . . . well, blood."

"No, that's not true," said Myrtle. "We just can't see beyond the blood itself. We can't see what's inside it, what makes it up."

"Maybe someday someone will be able to figure that out," said Jake.

"Maybe," said Myrtle. "But for now, gentlemen, I believe the celebration must come to an end for it is time for me to depart."

She held her glass up for Jake to retrieve it.

"That is, if I might get someone to transport me home," she added.

"You're ready to call it a night already?" asked Henri.

"Unlike you gentlemen, I have a regular schedule of hours I am obligated to keep," said Myrtle, getting up from her chair. "Besides, I have a wedding to get ready for."

"You're getting married?" asked Teddy.

"Which one of these lucky guys is it?" asked Jake, his eyes going first to Henri then to George.

It was no secret around town that both of them were after Myrtle.

"What makes you think it's either of them?" asked Myrtle, grinning.

"Then maybe I still have a chance?" said Teddy.

"Oh, Teddy, if I were but ten years younger," said Myrtle, laughing.

"So, when do we find out?" asked Jake.

"You read the *Rapids,* Mr. McIntyre?"

"I do."

"Daisy's putting my engagement notice in Wednesday's edition. Then everyone in town will know."

"What if you change your mind between now and then?" asked Henri.

"She said if I did, it would be my obituary running because she'd strangle me with her own two hands."

CHAPTER THIRTY-NINE

Myrtle stood in the open doorway eyeing the aisle before her that led to the chancel area. It seemed to stretch on forever.

Waiting for her there was the closest thing she had to a family: Daisy, Henri, Pierre, and Mrs. Darling, people with whom she had been sharing a home for the past three years, and the other members of the wedding party.

The overflow of guests, townsfolk as well as students and staff from the college, people she knew from the library, were on their feet, their eyes fixed on her.

"Shall we?"

Myrtle turned to look at the man standing next to her who had just spoken and whose arm she held.

It seemed strange, she thought, that she had known Thomas Wickersham longer than any of the people now gathered in this church for her wedding—though not by much.

The last time he'd been in town he painted Myrtle's portrait. She still had it but kept it packed safely away as it was a bit too revealing for anyone else to see it.

On his many visits over the last year and a half he had

made it clear to Myrtle that he had grown increasingly fond of her.

Today he had unexpectedly appeared in the sacristy moments after Daisy's departure.

*****

"Thomas!" cried Myrtle. "What are you doing here?"

"I heard it was your wedding day. I wanted to give you the opportunity to change your mind and run away with me."

Myrtle laughed and hugged him. "Dear Thomas. I fear you have made the trip in vain. I have every intention of going through with it."

"That's what Daisy said. I met her out in the hallway. Then she said something very strange."

"What was that?"

"She said her money had been on me."

Myrtle laughed. "Yes, she and Pierre had a bet as to whom I would choose to be my husband."

"So Pierre won the bet," said Thomas.

Myrtle smiled. "No, they both lost. Now, since you are here, you may be of service to me."

She had planned to walk down the aisle unattended. But the closer the moment got, the less sure she was she could make it on her own. She asked Thomas to escort her and he readily agreed.

*****

Now here they were, a church full of guests waiting for them to make their move.

"Shall we?" Thomas asked again.

Myrtle nodded. "We shall."

From her perch in the choir loft in the balcony above where Myrtle and Thomas now stood, Hannah Järvinen kept a watchful eye on the aisle below. Hannah had served as the organist at St. Barbara's since the instrument had been installed six months after the church was built and had played for over three hundred weddings, most of them mine workers and their mail-order brides.

When she saw Myrtle and Thomas emerge from under the balcony overhang she breathed a sigh of relief. Today would not have been the first time a bride had gotten cold feet. She watched as they made their way down the aisle. When they stopped in front of Father Fabian, Hannah gave the music a final flourish and raised her hands from the keyboard.

Father Fabian's sonorous voice filled the room.

"Dearly Beloved . . ."

*****

Forty-five minutes later Myrtle stood facing the man who, in minutes, would be her husband.

Ten minutes ago her mind had begun to wander from the proceedings. Try as she might, she couldn't get the idea of the reception awaiting her and her guests—and, of course, her husband—across the street in the basement of the Lutheran Church out of her mind.

Her mouth watered at the thought of the salmiakki, ice cream that tasted like salty black licorice. She had sampled it the first time three years ago at the ice cream social to which George had invited her.

"And do you..."

Myrtle's thoughts were jerked back to the present.

Better concentrate.

"...Myrtle Esmerelda Tully take Henri Fernandez de la Cruz to be your husband, to have and to hold from this day forward; for better, for worse, for richer, for poorer, in sickness and in health, to love, cherish, and obey, till death you do part, according to God's Holy Law?"

Myrtle looked into Henri's eyes.

He was beaming.

"I do," she said as a wide grin spread across her face, "…except for that obey part."

"Be that as it may," said Father Fabian, raising his voice in order to be heard over the laughter ringing out through the sanctuary,

"I now pronounce you man and wife."

ABOUT THE AUTHOR

A retired Lutheran minister, Kenn has served congregations in Indiana, Kentucky, and Missouri. In 2000 he sold his wedding business in Maui, Hawaii, and retired to Lower Northern Michigan (Ernest Hemingway country), where he and his wife, Judy, also a retired minister, both in their eighties, along with their fourteen-year-old dog, Louie (fifty percent Beagle, twenty-five percent Samoyed, twenty-five percent Old English Sheepdog) grow gracefully old together, living the good life in their cabin on Deer Lake.

The Booker Falls Mystery Series
Strangled in the Stacks
Trifecta of Murder
Paint the Librarian Dead

Other Books by Kenn Grimes
Camptown .One Hundred and Fifty Years of Stories from Camptown, Kentucky
The Other Side of Yesterday
Ancestors
To Save Us All from Satan's Power
The Whipping Post

Made in the USA
Middletown, DE
19 July 2021